# FITTING IN . . .

"You make me sick! You think you're so great. All you do is put people down like you're better than everybody else. Well, you're not! Not one bit. I'll take my friends in Nueva Beach over you Palm Beach preppies any day! I'm outta here."

Quinn stomped noisily across the patio and into the house. A moment later the sound of her bike on the gravel driveway reached the group still standing shocked and silent by the pool. Then everybody started talking at once.

"That little creep!" Jesse said, breaking the silence.

"What a jerk!" Stephanie agreed.

Mimi tried to soothe Cara. "You can't listen to people like her. What a loser."

Cara's pale eyes were very dark. She folded her arms across he chest. "How *dare* she!" Cara said in a high, icy voice. "Quinn McNair is going to be very sorry that she ever set foot in Palm Beach Prep," she added dramatically as she hoisted herself out of the pool.

# New Girl in Town

PALM BEACH
P R E P

Created by
## Carol Q.
## Sansevere

LYNX BOOKS
New York

PALM BEACH PREP: NEW GIRL IN TOWN

ISBN: 1-55802-200-7

First Printing/March 1989

Editorial contributions by E. M. Rees

This book is published by Lynx Books, a division of Lynx Communications, Inc., 41 Madison Avenue, New York, New York, 10010. The name "Lynx" and the logo consisting of a stylized head of a lynx are a trademarks of Lynx Communications, Inc.

Printed in the United States of America

0 9 8 7 6 5 4 3 2 1

*For Jennifer Gerson*

# New Girl in Town

PALM BEACH
PREP

# CHAPTER

## 1

"Clones," Quinn McNair mumbled in a voice unusually gravelly and deep for a twelve-year-old girl. Somehow, saying the word out loud made her feel better. It helped quiet the first-day-at-a-new-school butterflies in her stomach a little. She'd awakened that morning feeling totally queasy, as if she'd swallowed her little brother's goldfish. The tall, red-haired girl glanced around the cafeteria of Palm Beach Preparatory School for Girls. It was nothing like the cafeteria at her old public school in Nueva Beach. Quinn tried to digest the fact that she was dressed exactly like every other girl in sight: blue and green kilt, navy-blue blazer, blue knee socks, and a boring white blouse. Well, clothes alone don't make a clone, Quinn thought, and felt rather pleased with coining the phrase. Besides, the dumb uniform helped

1

hide the fact that Quinn was not rich, like most of the girls in the school. She was only at PBP because she had won a scholarship.

"Hey, you're the new girl—Quinn McNair," a friendly voice said, interrupting her thoughts. Quinn turned around. She had to look down a little because the girl who had spoken was sort of short. But her eyes were dark and sparkling, and in spite of her uniform, she didn't look quite like the other clones.

"How do you know my name?" Quinn asked, totally surprised that someone was being so friendly. In Nueva Beach, where Quinn lived, her friends called the girls who went to school here "Palm Beach Preppies." After one morning, Quinn could understand why. No one had even bothered to say hello, or ask her her name.

"I'm in Miss Gordon's sixth-grade homeroom with you," the dark-haired girl explained, trying to clip a bright red barrette into her tangle of black curls. "Besides, you're the only new girl in the class." She sounded excited by the fact as she looked Quinn up and down and grinned.

Quinn would have grinned back, but she was too shocked. "I am?" she asked, the butterflies in her stomach starting to flutter again. "The *only* new girl?" Quinn knew the school wasn't very big, but she'd hoped there'd be at least one other new girl in the class.

"The last new girl in our class came last year,"

the other girl said and frowned. "Mimi Roth from New York—"

"Yuck and double yuck!" said a breathy voice from just behind Quinn. She turned around. She found herself face-to-face with an incredibly pretty girl who looked almost like a doll—all big blue eyes and pale blond hair. The girl sniffed the air and wrinkled her model-like face in disgust.

Quinn suddenly felt very sorry for Mimi Roth, whomever she might be. Obviously, no one liked her very much.

The blond girl sniffed again, and said dramatically, "I *hate* Sloppy Joes!"

"Sloppy Joes?" Quinn repeated, looking confused. So Mimi Roth wasn't the object of the blond girl's disgust. But Quinn's favorite lunch was.

"It smells disgusting!" the blond girl exclaimed and looked right into Quinn's eyes. She seemed to take it for granted that Quinn thought so, too. "Yuck and double yuck!" she repeated.

Before Quinn could tell her that she loved Sloppy Joes, the dark-haired girl let out a string of Spanish words. "Esme," she continued, tweeking one of the blond girl's five pale braids, "stop sounding so tragic. You know we always have Sloppy Joes on the first day of school. Just because we have a new cafeteria doesn't mean we're not going to have the same old food."

"Last year's food, I bet," Esme said grumpily

3

as she patted her braids back into place. The short girl laughed and pushed her thick, black curls off her face.

"What else would Heartburn give us for lunch?" she said, and winked broadly at Quinn. Then she noticed the puzzled look on Quinn's face. "That's what we call the headmistress, Mrs. Hartman."

Quinn's confusion gave way to a delighted grin. "So Flo does have a nickname."

"Flo!" the other two girls exclaimed in unison.

"Well, Florence is her name, isn't it? Florence Hartman?" Quinn retorted.

"As sure as mine's Alicia Antona," the dark-haired girl confirmed, stopping to hand a tray first to Quinn and then to Esme. "And hers is Esme Farrell."

"But no one calls Heartburn 'Flo,' " Esme said, her blue eyes opening very wide. "Ever!"

Quinn decided that Esme was kind of wimpy, the exact opposite of Quinn, who prided herself on being tough. "She couldn't hear me," Quinn said defensively, wondering what made Alicia want to be friends with an airhead like Esme.

"*Las paredes oyen,*" Alicia warned dramatically.

"The walls are listening?" Quinn said as she tried to translate Alicia's Cuban Spanish. She thought for a moment, and then said, "I've got it—the walls have ears. That's what you meant, isn't it?"

Alicia looked surprised. *"Se habla Espanol?"* she asked, looking disappointed when Quinn shook her head.

"Last year I took beginning Spanish, but I don't know very much. I can understand a lot more than I can speak."

"We all have to study French here until high school," Alicia informed Quinn as the cafeteria line inched forward. "Then we can take any language we want. But anyway, I wouldn't let Heartburn hear you call her Flo."

Quinn shrugged in a way that made it perfectly clear that she didn't care what either the walls or Heartburn herself might hear.

"Hey, there's Nicole," Alicia said suddenly to Esme. "I bet she headed straight from assembly to the stables. She probably brought carrots for Simon," Alicia continued, and turned back to Quinn. "Simon's her horse, by the way. You haven't met Nicole yet, have you?"

"No, you're the first person I've met," Quinn admitted.

At the sight of the brown-haired girl headed purposefully toward their spot on the line, Quinn thought she looked exactly like one of the Palm Beach preppies her friends in Nueva Beach had warned her about. Nicole's smooth hair was drawn into a low ponytail at the base of her long neck and was tied with a blue ribbon. Her uniform was immaculately ironed—even the cuffs on her socks looked pressed. She looked, Quinn decided, as if she'd walked off the pages of a preppy catalog, from the tips of her shiny brown loafers to the top of her shiny brown hair.

"Nicole," Alicia said, beckoning eagerly to her friend. "This is the new girl, the one I told you about during assembly. Quinn, this is Nicole Whitcomb. Nicole, this is Quinn McNair."

Nicole looked from Alicia to Quinn to Esme and back to Quinn again.

"Hi," she said in a quiet voice, not unfriendly, but not friendly either.

Nicole held back a little before grabbing a tray and stepping in front of Esme. Then she turned around and stared at Quinn.

Quinn felt the color rush to her lightly freckled face as Nicole very slowly looked her up and down. Her gaze moved from Quinn's rolled-down blue knee socks to her turned-up collar and rolled-up blazer sleeves, finally resting on the silver key hanging from one of her ears. Nicole's high forehead creased in a deep and definite frown.

Quinn's face went from pink to red. She was right, this was a real Palm Beach preppy whose standards Nueva Beach-born Quinn definitely did not meet. Quinn didn't wait to hear whatever Nicole was about to say. She didn't need her insults spelled out for her.

"Nice to meet you," Quinn said sarcastically, addressing Nicole directly. "You must be the head

6

preppy of the Palm Beach Prep welcoming committee." Quinn turned her back on the three girls and pushed her way up the line as far away from them as she could get. The last thing Quinn McNair needed in her life was an airhead and a Palm Beach preppy.

"What's the matter with her?" Quinn heard Nicole say. "She's going to get in trouble, looking like that. Heartburn's going to give her detention."

"What did we do?" Esme asked, looking down at Alicia with a puzzled expression on her face. "Did Heartburn put Nicole on a welcoming committee? How come I never heard about it?"

"She was kidding, Es," Alicia explained.

"Don't worry, Alicia. You were just trying to be friendly. After all, she's new here. It's going to be hard for her to fit in," Nicole predicted.

Three tables away, Cara Knowles studied Quinn intently as she stomped away from Alicia, Nicole, and Esme. "Who's that girl?" she asked, pointing in Quinn's direction. Cara, reigning queen of the sixth-grade class, had to know everything about everybody. All heads at her crowded table turned to look in Quinn's direction.

"Oh, her?" replied Cara's best friend, Jesse Langdon. "She's in my homeroom."

"She's a brain," Patty Porter, known as "The Mouth," informed the table, pushing her tortoiseshell glasses up on her nose.

"Really?" Cara said, looking back at Quinn. "What's her name? And how do you know she's a brain? We haven't had any classes yet."

"Her name's Quinn McNair."

Cara digested this information as she twirled a few strands of her silky dark-blond hair around her finger.

"Well," Patty explained, "she won that big essay contest. You know, the one about how you'd put an end to war if you were President of the United States."

Across the table, Stephanie Barns whistled under her breath. "I remember now. Her picture was in the paper last month." Stephanie stood up and shielded her eyes from the sun pouring through the glass-brick wall on the other side of the cafeteria. "Why is she wearing her uniform that way? If Heartburn was patrolling, she'd be in major trouble."

"I know," Jesse agreed. "And anyway, she looks like a slob."

"I like how she's wearing her uniform," Cara announced dramatically with a toss of her blond hair. Her light-blue eyes looked at Jesse, Patty, and Stephanie in turn. "It's cool." Cara wasn't quite as sure as she sounded. Quinn's out-of-uniform blue slouch socks and funky black shoes might seem cool, but she knew exactly what Heartburn would think of the key dangling from one of Quinn's ears.

"I don't know, Cara," Jesse said, shaking her short light-brown hair from side to side.

Cara let out an exasperated sigh. Sometimes her friends had absolutely no imagination. Any girl who walked away from Alicia & co. couldn't be so bad, no matter how she dressed. All five of Cara's group followed Quinn's progress out the cafeteria's door. They watched her pause at the edge of the patio and look around. Not seeming to mind what happened to her blue-and-green-plaid uniform kilt, she plopped down and kicked off her shoes. A minute later, the socks followed.

Jesse gasped.

"She's barefoot!" Patty announced in a shocked voice.

Stephanie giggled. "Good for her." She stretched out her long athletic legs and added, "As long as she doesn't get caught."

"You know what? I'm going to meet her," Cara declared as she pushed back her chair. "See you guys later," she called over her shoulder as she walked across the crowded lunchroom, pleased by the shocked expressions on all of her friends' faces.

Quinn seemed to sense Cara's presence and looked up from her book.

"My name's Cara Knowles," Cara began in what she hoped was a friendly voice.

Quinn didn't crack a smile, though it occurred to her that if she didn't start trying to make

9

friends, it would be a long year. "Are you in sixth grade, too?" Quinn asked.

"Yeah," Cara replied, "and I hear you're in my best friend Jesse's homeroom. You're Quinn McNair, right?"

Reluctantly, Cara sat down beside Quinn on the grass, praying that there were no lizards around. Lizards, much to her disgust, were all over the place in Southern Florida—especially at The Palms, the huge estate where Cara had lived all her life.

"How long have you been at Palm Beach Prep?" Quinn asked, tucking her book inside her black knapsack, which was covered with buttons of her favorite musicians.

"Since first grade," Cara replied. "How'd you end up at the Swamp, Quinn?"

Quinn looked at Cara. "The what?"

"The Swamp," she said, pausing dramatically. "That's what we call the school. The land used to be an old swamp until some rich old guy drained it to build his wife a mansion—"

Quinn leaned forward. "Was the wife young? What did she look like? Sounds romantic."

"Well, I don't think it was exactly romantic," Cara said slowly, racking her brain. It had been ages since she'd thought about it. "They had a daughter, who was probably pretty and stuff like that, and then one day she disappeared."

"She wandered off," Quinn said as she made

up her own version of the tale easily. "In the dead of night, the moon was full and she was searching for her lover. . . ." She looked at Cara with a dreamy expression. "How old was she? Like our age, or sixteen, or—"

Cara interrupted. "At least sixteen—I mean she was dating this guy . . . and then . . . they never found her again."

"No body!" Quinn exclaimed. This was getting better and better. "That means," she said, lowering her voice, "there must be a ghost!"

"A ghost?" Cara echoed. Suddenly the bell rang. She started to laugh. "I never heard about a ghost, Quinn. Where'd you get that idea?"

Quinn smiled sheepishly. "It sort of made sense. I love ghost stories. I might even write them when I grow up."

"So maybe you'll write for the paper. I'm the editor, you know."

"You have a newspaper?" Quinn asked excitedly. "I'd love to be on it."

"Speaking of newspapers, I heard there was a picture of you in the paper over the summer for something you wrote," Cara replied sweetly.

"Oh, that," Quinn said, shrugging it off. "I just love to write. I'll write anything. That's actually why I'm here—for the English department."

"Really?" Cara enthused as she digested this information. "I guess we should get to class. We

11

can talk about the paper later. By the way, are you doing anything after school?"

"I'm not doing anything today. I was just going to bike home and—"

"Great, 'cause it's my birthday and I'm having a party. Do you want to come?"

"Happy birthday!" Quinn exclaimed as she slapped Cara heartily on the back.

Cara reeled a little, then straightened her jacket.

"Okay. . ." Quinn replied, "but I don't have a present."

"Don't worry about it," Cara said warmly. "It'll give you a chance to meet the *very best* people at PBP."

# CHAPTER
## 2

At three o'clock that afternoon, after she had been introduced to all of Cara's friends, Quinn hopped on her black boy's ten-speed bike and began pumping her thin legs as hard as she could.

"Race ya!" Quinn hollered over her shoulder to the girls behind her.

"She's going to race?" Patty asked, blinking in disbelief.

"On that?" Jesse exclaimed as she glanced down at her shiny new red Peugot.

"I'm surprised it moves at all," Stephanie added. "Would you believe that she and her brother actually put it together from some bikes they found in a junkyard?"

"She's got a lot to learn about the rules around here," Cara said firmly, shaking her head.

"Really," Mimi agreed. "It took me months to

13

get it all straight." Mimi had moved to Palm Beach last year from Long Island. She was the newest member of Cara's clique.

Stephanie looked after Quinn as she disappeared beyond a bend in the shrub-lined drive. As soon as Stephanie rode through the open wrought-iron entrance gate and out onto the street, she tore after her.

Quinn had stopped at the corner. She looked back at the other girls to see what had happened to them.

"Follow me!" Stephanie screamed as she zoomed past Quinn.

After a few blocks, the athletic Stephanie had to struggle to stay ahead. The next thing she knew, Quinn was waving as she passed her. Patty was amazed that Quinn was winning. "Do you believe it? That hunk of junk can really move."

Cara was annoyed. She was taking *her* friends to *her* birthday party, and Quinn was getting all the attention. "I think racing is really dumb," she said, turning to Jesse. "When are they going to grow up?"

Jesse nodded. "I know."

The Knowles's estate, The Palms, faced the ocean. Quinn skidded to a halt at the gatepost, and Stephanie pulled up barely a second later.

"Why'd you stop? We're not there yet," Stephanie said as she wiped the sweat off her forehead.

14

"This is Cara's house?" Quinn asked in astonishment.

Stephanie looked at Quinn. "Well, yeah."

Quinn closed her mouth. She realized that she was gaping, but she couldn't help it. The stucco and red-tiled mansion at the end of the curved, palm-lined driveway looked like a country club, not a home.

Finally, the other girls caught up and rode through the gates. Quinn followed slowly, taking in the in-ground sprinklers too numerous to count and thought of her father watering their lawn with the garden hose on Sunday morning.

The girls parked their bikes and followed Cara up the semicircular steps to the massive wooden front door. Quinn was amazed by the columns. They were huge and looked as if they belonged somewhere in Greece. She was startled when the door was opened by a maid dressed in a black-and-white uniform like she'd seen in movies. The maid, whose name was Dora, led them into a huge room with a wall of windows looking out toward the back lawn and the ocean.

Quinn couldn't believe it. A jungle of real trees lined the wall beneath the picture window. Quinn had never seen trees growing in a house before. All the furniture was white, even the rug. At Quinn's house, nothing white stayed that way with her brothers around.

"Would you like a soda?" Dora asked Quinn.

"Here, let me help," Quinn said, and took the tray out of the surprised Dora's hands. "I'll bring these around for you," she volunteered.

"Quinn!" Cara hissed as Quinn set the tray down on the coffee table. "What are you *doing*?"

"Helping," she said as she grabbed a soda.

"But we're not supposed to help," Jesse said haughtily. "Everyone knows that."

Quinn bristled at Jesse's comment. "I always offer to help when I go to my friends' houses," she said defensively, wondering what the big deal was.

"Listen," Cara interrupted, "let's go to my room and change." She turned to Quinn. "Oh, Quinn, do you have anything to change into?"

"No, I thought Mrs. Hartman said we couldn't wear anything but uniforms or riding clothes on campus—unless we had special permission."

"We can't. Heartburn's uniform-to-be-worn-five-blocks-or-less-around-the-school rule!" Stephanie called from the playroom door. "That's why we always bring clothes to change into when there's a party."

"Do you want to borrow something?" Cara asked less than invitingly.

"No, thanks," Quinn replied and contented herself with shrugging off her jacket and tossing it onto a chair. She watched Dora put out several plates of interesting-looking tiny sandwiches. Quinn popped one in her mouth, then walked around the room to look at everything. A pile of presents heaped on a corner table caught her eye. As she moved toward them, the other girls returned, Cara in the lead. Cara sat down in a chair and smoothed a nonexistent wrinkle out of her crisp white shorts.

"Too bad Paula Evans couldn't be here," Stephanie remarked, reaching over Jesse to grab a couple of sandwiches.

"Too bad *I* couldn't spend my birthday in Paris with Paula," Cara countered. "Imagine that lucky creep getting to spend an entire summer in France."

"She even gets to miss a week of school," Mimi added.

"So does Keri Johnson," Patty reminded them. She walked over to the glass-fronted cabinet that housed Cara's collection of record albums, compact disks, and cassettes. "She got to spend the summer in Italy." Patty dropped down to the floor and rifled through the albums. She was right next to Quinn, but seemed totally unaware of her existence.

"Italy's not such a big deal," Jesse said and shrugged. "Though I bet you ten-to-one that Keri will come back pretending Italian's her native language."

"She's such a snob. I mean, the way she dresses. And I bet she got tons of new clothes," Stephanie added.

"Do you like Michael Jackson, Quinn?" Cara asked as she slipped a CD out of its case. Quinn couldn't believe Cara's stereo system. Her brother Sean would flip if he saw it.

"He's okay, but I'm really into reggae," Quinn replied. "My brother hooked me on it. He's in a reggae band. Actually, they're totally psyched because they're playing at Nueva High's homecoming dance next month."

"Nueva High? Why would they play over there?" Cara asked, wrinkling her nose in distaste.

"Why not? That's where they go to school," Quinn replied, confused.

"But Nueva Beach is dangerous. I mean, lots of crimes happen there—"

"I live there, Cara," Quinn interrupted, her voice raised so that all the other girls turned to look at her.

"You *live* in Nueva Beach?" Patty questioned, her eyebrows arched in surprise.

"I've never been there," Jesse added, looking sideways at Cara.

Before Quinn could respond, Dora appeared in the doorway. "Aren't you going to open your presents, Cara?" she asked. "Why don't you take them out to the pool, and I'll get the cake."

"What a great idea, Dora. Come on, guys," Cara said as she got up and walked through the French doors opening onto the patio.

Quinn felt Cara's eyes on her when Dora disappeared to get the cake. She forced herself to pull up a lawn chair like the other girls and not offer to help in the kitchen. Quinn pushed her shirt sleeves up above her elbows. She couldn't help but wish she'd brought her bathing suit. But then, she never expected to be here in the first place. The girls kept gossiping about people she didn't know, and she was bored. She turned to Mimi, who had hardly said a word all afternoon. "So, are you on the paper?"

"What?" Mimi asked distractedly, trying to hear who it was who had spent the summer at a fat camp.

"The newspaper. Do you write for it?" Quinn tried again.

"No, not just anybody can be on Cara's paper," Mimi replied earnestly.

"Why are you talking about the paper?" Stephanie interrupted. "This is a party. We're not in school anymore."

Quinn rolled her eyes and looked out toward the ocean. These girls were too much. Cara presided like a princess over the stack of presents. Quinn hadn't seen so many gifts in one place since Christmas. As Cara tore off the wrapping paper, the conversation turned first to clothes and then to hair.

"Did you see Esme today? Didn't she look stupid with all those braids?" Stephanie said, leaning back in her chair and closing her eyes against the sun.

"I see she's still tight with Nicole and Alicia," Jesse commented.

As Cara finished admiring each gift, Jesse took it from her and added it to the growing tower piled on a nearby chair. Already there were several new tennis outfits, three videos—including one of Michael Jackson live at a London concert— and an assortment of jewelry and hair clips.

"Esme's an airhead," Cara said flatly. "So what if she's a professional model."

"I heard she's going to be in *Seventeen*," Patty reported.

"I'll believe it when I see it," Cara countered, picking up the last present.

"It's from my father," she exclaimed. Sensing Quinn's eyes on her, Cara looked up. "My father's in Europe," she explained. "He's very important, so he's always busy. But he never forgets my birthday." She bit her lip and pushed her perfectly blunt-cut hair away from her cheek.

Like the other girls, Quinn leaned forward, eager to see what was inside.

"Ooooh!" Cara shrieked.

"What is it?" everyone asked as they crowded around Cara.

Quinn peered down at the plastic watch Cara was holding up for everyone to see. It was the tackiest thing Quinn had ever seen. It could practically blind someone, it was so bright—tons of neon colors. While everyone was "oohing" and "aahing," Quinn remained silent as she stared at the watch. She finally tore her eyes away from it and looked up to see Jesse watching her, an unsmiling look on her face.

"All right, guys, let's go swimming now," Cara commanded, peeling off her shorts and T-shirt. She adjusted the strap on her hot-pink tank suit and backflipped off the diving board. The other girls followed her into the pool.

Hot and bored, Quinn walked around the pool. A lawn mower rounded the corner, and she did a double take. The guy on the tractor looked very familiar. As he got closer, she saw that it was her brother's best friend, Ricky. She ran into his path, and he cut the engine.

"What are *you* doing here?" they both asked at once.

"My dad's the Knowles's gardener," Ricky explained as he pushed his sunglasses to the top of his dark curly hair. He looked Quinn up and down and started to laugh. "Hey, I heard you were going to that preppy school. But do you really have to dress like that?"

"I know, it's the worst," Quinn agreed. "Hey, don't you have to get back to work? I wouldn't want to get you in trouble," she teased. "Sean would never forgive me if you lost your job and he had to treat for the rest of the semester down at Palmetto Pete's."

"Speaking of trouble," Ricky replied as he rolled his eyes and gestured to the crowd of girls behind her.

"What do you mean?" she asked.

"Nothing. Don't worry about it. Well, I'd better get back to work. See you later, Quinn," he said as he started the tractor engine.

"You *know* him!" Cara exclaimed, squeezing the water out of her hair when Quinn returned to the pool.

"Yeah," Quinn said with a shrug. "Ricky's my brother Sean's best friend. He's the drummer in that band I told you about."

"But he's a gardener," Cara said in disgust.

"No one I know is friends with gardeners," Jesse added.

"Really, Quinn," Cara said icily, "we're not friends with the people who work for us."

Quinn sputtered, too angry to reply. The frustration she'd felt all afternoon, listening to everyone's snide empty gossip about clothes, about hair, about other girls not around and unable to defend themselves, began to boil up inside her. At Cara's sarcastic, belittling tone, Quinn straightened her shoulders and let loose her Irish temper.

"You make me sick! You think you're so great. All you do is put people down like you're better than everybody else. Well, you're not! Not one bit.

I'll take my friends in Nueva Beach over you Palm Beach preppies any day! I'm outta here."

Quinn stomped noisily across the patio and into the house. A moment later the sound of her bike on the gravel driveway reached the group still standing shocked and silent by the pool. Then everybody started talking at once.

"That little creep!" Jesse said, breaking the silence.

"What a jerk!" Stephanie agreed.

Mimi tried to soothe Cara. "You can't listen to people like her. What a loser."

Cara's pale eyes were very dark. She folded her arms across her chest. "How *dare* she!" Cara said in a high icy voice. "Quinn McNair is going to be very sorry that she ever set foot in Palm Beach Prep," she added dramatically as she hoisted herself out of the pool.

# CHAPTER 3

"Maybe I didn't understand you, Mrs. Hartman," Quinn said as she faced the headmistress across her massive wooden desk.

Mrs. Hartman glanced up over her glasses and smiled at Quinn. Quinn stared back. "It's really quite simple, Quinn," Mrs. Hartman said as she tucked an imaginary hair back into her bun and explained her plan again. "Since you're here on scholarship, I realized that you might need a little, shall we say, additional financial aid."

Quinn struggled to hold her temper. She wanted to get Mrs. Hartman's story straight. She knew that sometimes she jumped to conclusions—actually often, more than sometimes. Quinn took a deep breath, forced herself to count to ten, then leaned forward a little and regarded the headmistress with serious blue eyes. "I thought the Emerson Scholarship was all the aid I could get."

"Yes, that is true, but as you don't come from the same economic background as many of the girls here—" She let the words hang in the air between them as a picture of Cara's house flashed through Quinn's mind.

Mrs. Hartman smiled again, if one could call the slight upward motion of her thin lips a smile. Quinn was sure she'd never have to worry about getting laugh lines. The headmistress stopped speaking and stared hard at Quinn. Quinn was puzzled, until she remembered something Mrs. Hartman had said in yesterday's assembly. "Palm Beach Prep Girls do not ever *slouch*." Quinn gulped and sat up straight in her chair.

Mrs. Hartman resumed speaking. "We have some paid tutoring jobs for students and there are some openings this semester. As you are bright and in financial need, I have already assigned you two students in English, and I thought perhaps another in history, though we don't want to work you too hard." Mrs. Hartman picked up a piece of paper on her desk and settled her glasses on her nose.

Quinn barely heard Mrs. Hartman's last words. Her cheeks were hot with humiliation and hurt pride. First Nicole, then Cara and her snobby little friends and now this.

"What makes you think I need tutoring jobs?"

Quinn exclaimed, too overwrought to think of what she was saying. "Just because I'm on scholarship, you think I need money? Well, I don't. And even if I needed it, I'd find a way of getting it myself." Quinn leaped to her feet and stared down at the startled Mrs. Hartman. Her blue eyes stung with tears, but Quinn held them back.

"Now, dear, there is no need to be embarrassed about your situation."

"I'm *not* embarrassed," Quinn said through clenched teeth. "It's everybody else in this school who thinks there's something wrong with mc because I'm not rich."

For an instant, Mrs. Hartman gaped at Quinn, unable to believe what she'd just heard. Then, an angry flush crept up her neck. "The first thing we learn when we come to Palm Beach Preparatory School for Girls is respect, Miss McNair. You will *not* speak to me in that tone of voice. You can think about your behavior in detention this afternoon. And you can also begin wearing your uniform properly. Roll down your sleeves at once, and fix your collar. And please note that you are not wearing regulation knee socks."

Quinn gritted her teeth and did as she was told. She yanked down her sleeves and turned down her collar.

"I will not tolerate behavior like this in the future," Mrs. Hartman reprimanded. "You are excused. Go back to class."

Later that afternoon in science class, Esme whispered to Alicia, "Did you hear about the new girl?" The room was in semidarkness as Miss Kent struggled to get the classroom VCR to work. At the moment, the four-foot TV screen embedded in one of the classroom walls was blank.

Alicia shook her head. "I only know Heartburn called her to the office during homeroom."

"But it's only the second day of school. What could she have done?" Nicole asked in surprise.

Esme pushed her long blond hair out of her eyes and glared first at Alicia and then at Nicole. "If you'd just shut up, I'd tell you. The Mouth told me that Quinn got detention."

"Detention!" Nicole exclaimed loudly. Nicole feared detention, especially from Mrs. Hartman, as a fate worse than death. Mrs. Hartman had been at PBP with Nicole's grandmother, and they were still the best of friends. Given a choice between detention and jumping into an alligator-infested swamp, Nicole would take the swamp any time.

"Miss Whitcomb?" Miss Kent said, interrupting their conversation. Nicole, whose secret ambition was to be a vet, was one of the teacher's favorite students. "Is something wrong?"

"Uh—no, Miss Kent," Nicole said, slumping down in her seat. She glared at Esme.

Esme continued whispering. "The Mouth said Quinn was incredibly rude at Cara's party yester-

27

day. Supposedly, she told them that they made her sick, and then left."

"But how would that get Quinn detention?" Alicia asked. "She must have done something else."

"I don't know," Esme replied.

"Poor Quinn," Alicia said sympathetically.

"Why 'Poor Quinn'?" Nicole interrupted. "She was so out of uniform yesterday, it's really not surprising."

"Well, I feel bad for her," Alicia retorted.

"Anyway, she looked cool and this uniform is the worst. You can't help it if *you* like it."

Later, three pairs of eyes watched Quinn as she stomped to her locker. Quinn struggled twice with the combination lock, then kicked the locker.

"She looks pretty upset," Jesse said.

Quinn finally yanked open her locker, threw in the books she was carrying and grabbed some others, then slammed the door shut. The locker bounced open again, and Quinn slammed it again. This time, it stuck. She stormed off, aware of the attention she was receiving from the other girls.

The warning bell rang. "Oh, I don't want to be late for Monsieur Delacroix's first French class," Cara said as she glanced at her wrist, then shrieked. "Oh, no! My new watch is gone!"

The other girls crowded closer. "Did you forget to put it on this morning?" Jesse asked.

"No," Cara insisted a little hysterically. "I'm sure I had it on when I ate breakfast. I remember looking at it and saying I was late and needed to get a ride with James to school."

Stephanie ran up to her locker and began to fiddle with the combination. "Hi, guys," she greeted her friends. At the horrified expression on Cara's face, she forgot all about her locker and whatever it was she wanted inside. "What's the matter? What happened?" she asked.

"Cara's new watch is missing," Jesse announced in a tragic tone of voice.

"You had it this morning. You showed it to me right before gym," Stephanie said with certainty. "I remember."

"You're right," Cara agreed, "I did have it then."

"Did you check your gym bag?" Patty suggested, then nervously eyed the hall. The crowd of girls changing classes had emptied out. They were surely going to be late for French now.

"Yes—no—I don't know." Cara raced over to her locker and opened it quickly. She pulled out her bag and dumped the contents on the floor. She sorted through the items and then shoved them back in again. She looked up, and her face was streaked with tears. "Oh, it's gone. I lost it. And it was from my father," she wailed.

Jesse dropped down next to Cara and helped her stuff the bag back into her locker. "Maybe you took it off in the bathroom when you washed your hands."

"I'd never take it off. Never!" Cara declared passionately. "But maybe I should check just to be sure. What if I never find it?" Cara wailed as the tears trickled down her cheeks. None of the other girls had ever seen her this distraught. Only Jesse knew how much Cara missed having her parents around, especially her father. But they were both into their careers and never seemed to have much time for their only daughter.

"Girls, shouldn't you be in class?" Mrs. Hartman's voice caused everyone to turn around.

"Oh, Mrs. Hartman," Jesse said and jumped up. "Cara's watch—the one her father gave her for her birthday—it's gone!"

"Gone?" the headmistress asked as she peered over the rim of her glasses. Her gaze softened as she watched Cara wipe the tears from her eyes. "Cara, have you looked for it, dear?"

"Oh, yes, Mrs. Hartman. I looked in my bag and my locker and—"

"She was on her way to the bathroom to look there," Patty informed the headmistress.

"Well, look carefully. And retrace your steps. Then, if you still can't find it, come to the office. Perhaps someone will have found it and turned it in."

"Yes, Mrs. Hartman," the girls chorused.

"Now, off to class, girls. Let me know if you find it, Cara," Mrs. Hartman said as she walked toward the office.

"But they won't find it," Cara cried, "because I didn't take it off. I know I didn't."

Jesse tried to soothe her. "Maybe you put it down and just can't remember what you did with it."

The last warning bell rang, and the girls hurried to get to French class, promising to meet afterward to look for the watch. "We've got to find it," Cara exclaimed as they reached the classroom.

"I'll help you look. We'll find it," Jesse reassured her.

After class, the girls retraced Cara's steps between gym class and her locker. The watch was nowhere to be found. "What could have happened to it?" Cara's voice was flat as she toyed aimlessly with the strap of her knapsack.

"Maybe it fell off your wrist?" Stephanie volunteered.

Cara shook her head. "I had it on extra tight this morning. I remember checking it. I can't believe it's gone."

"We're going to check the bathroom again, Cara," Patty said as she and Stephanie began to walk down the hall.

Jesse wrinkled her forehead and watched them go. She looked down the aisle toward Cara's locker. "Maybe somebody took it."

"Who would do that?" Cara asked disbelievingly.

"I don't know. But if you've looked everywhere and can't find it, what else could have happened to it?"

Cara thought for a moment. "Maybe you're

31

right, Jesse," she agreed. "But who would steal something around here?"

"Well," Jesse began hesitantly, "you know, I didn't think anything of it yesterday, but when you were opening your presents and you got to the watch, I noticed Quinn was really staring. She couldn't take her eyes off of it."

"Quinn?" Cara asked in surprise. "You think Quinn stole my watch?"

Just then, Patty and Stephanie returned. "What are you guys talking about?" Patty asked curiously. It was obvious that she had heard the tail end of their conversation. "Quinn took your watch?"

Cara looked at Jesse and said, "Patty, we were just talking about what might have happened. We didn't say Quinn took it."

"But you think she might have?" Stephanie asked.

"Anybody might have," Jesse said bluntly, "but Quinn really stared at Cara's watch yesterday when she first opened the package. I saw her."

"Well, we didn't say Quinn took it," Cara said directly to Patty. She had seen that intense look on The Mouth's face before, and she wasn't sure she wanted this all over school.

Patty didn't look very convinced, but changed the subject anyway. "There was nothing in the bathroom, Cara."

Cara sighed. Maybe Jesse was right. Where else could her watch be?

# CHAPTER

## 4

The next morning, Alicia detoured to the bathroom off the new student lounge before heading to her first class. Whistling a happy tune, she checked her reflection in the mirror, then went into the last stall against the wall. No sooner had she closed the door than a group of girls came in, chattering loudly. At the familiar whiny sound of Mimi Roth's voice, Alicia pricked up her ears.

"So, Patty, has Cara found her watch yet?"

"No," Patty informed the other girl.

"I wonder what happened to it," Mimi asked.

"Well," Patty said to Stephanie, "I guess we can trust her, Steph." Then she turned to Mimi. "Cara and Jesse think Quinn stole the watch," she said, and then paused dramatically, pleased to pass along such juicy gossip. "In fact, Cara stopped

33

looking for it. She says there's no reason to, so she must be pretty certain."

Stephanie's voice broke in. "Well, like Jesse told Cara, who else could have taken it? Besides, everyone knows about Quinn."

"Knows what?" Mimi asked, confused.

Alicia pressed her ear to the door of the stall and listened carefully. Were her own feelings about Quinn so off the mark?

"That she comes from Nueva Beach, and has all these brothers—" Stephanie began.

"Brothers?" Mimi said, sounding interested.

Inside the stall, Alicia was interested, too. She didn't know Quinn had brothers. She wondered how old Quinn's brothers were and if they all had red hair.

"This has nothing to do with Quinn's brothers," Patty broke in. "Cara's watch is gone, and she's sure that Quinn took it."

"Can she prove it?" Mimi asked, sounding doubtful.

"The point is," Patty added, "that until Quinn McNair got here, nothing had ever been missing around this school."

"Well, I lost my new Prince racket once—"

"Mimi, you lost it. No one stole it," Patty pointed out. "And no one's turned in Cara's watch at the office. She checked three times already. She's sure Quinn took it."

Alicia closed her eyes and took a deep breath. Poor Quinn, she thought.

Mimi's reply to that comment was cut off by the closing of the bathroom door. Alicia waited until she heard the girls' footsteps die off down the hall, then she poked her head out of the stall. "Those little creeps. They're not sure Quinn stole the watch. Now they're probably going to get her in big trouble," Alicia exclaimed out loud and shook her head in disgust at the door. Mimi's high-pitched giggle filtered back toward the bathroom. Alicia waited a moment longer, to make sure they wouldn't know she had overheard what they'd said. Then she went out into the hall. She checked both directions, then bolted up the stairs toward her classroom.

After class and throughout the morning, it was obvious that somebody hadn't kept quiet about the conversation in the bathroom. Alicia didn't think Patty could hold in a rumor like this for very long without bursting.

"Did you hear that Quinn stole Cara's watch?" Alicia heard one girl exclaim.

"Really? I wondered what happened to it. Cara's not the type to lose anything," another countered.

And later on, Alicia began to get really worried for Quinn. "Quinn was in my last class, and I think she's going to get into trouble. She was called to the office, she heard Miss Madden tell Virginia Choy."

"Patty thinks Quinn's going to get expelled. She doesn't even think Quinn will be in school tomorrow!" Anne Marie Hayes whispered.

Alicia had a few minutes before she had to head out to the first riding session of the year. She couldn't stop thinking about Quinn's problem. There was no proof that Quinn stole the watch, but there was also no proof that Quinn *didn't* steal the watch. Well, at least Alicia could make life as miserable for Cara as she was making it for Quinn. In the last few years, Alicia had seen Cara do some of the meanest things to people who got on her bad side. As she started down the path to the stables, Alicia suddenly knew exactly what she was going to do first.

Quinn gave her knee socks one last tug as she stood in front of Mrs. Hartman's desk. This was becoming a familiar place. At least she was wearing regulation knee socks today. She waited a moment for the headmistress to notice that she was there. Finally, Quinn cleared her throat.

Mrs. Hartman looked up and straightened the jacket of her navy blue tailored suit and gave Quinn a long, hard look. "A very serious matter has come to my attention."

Quinn frowned. She didn't know what Heartburn was talking about, but after her last experience, she didn't dare ask.

"A valuable watch belonging to a member of

36

your class is missing. I called you in to ask whether you know anything about it."

Quinn relaxed a little. "Me?" she asked, tapping her chest with her finger, remembering too late that she had forgotten to turn down the collar of her blouse. Hastily, she straightened her shirt, and was relieved that for once she'd remembered to roll down her jacket sleeves.

"Cara Knowles—" Mrs. Hartman began.

"Cara?" Quinn interrupted. "It's Cara's watch that's missing? I don't know anything about it, except that it's so bright that it looks like it glows in the dark."

"No one asked for your opinion of the stolen property, Quinn," Mrs. Hartman said icily. "It has come to my attention that there is talk that you had something to do with it."

Quinn's face turned red. "You think *I* stole Cara's watch?" Quinn could barely get the words out. "Are you kidding me? Why in the world would I want her watch? I have two of my own," she said as she pushed up her blazer sleeve to display the two plastic watches she wore on her left wrist.

"I didn't accuse you of anything, Quinn," Mrs. Hartman replied.

"Well, I bet you didn't call anybody else in to see if they knew anything about the watch. Just because my locker's right next to Cara's, and somebody is spreading rumors about me, you think I took it. Well, I always thought people were innocent until proven guilty. But I guess that's not the way it is at Palm Beach Preparatory School for Girls!"

"That will be enough, Miss McNair. I have already spoken to you about this kind of outburst. I asked you a simple question. Do you, or do you not, know anything about the watch?"

Quinn was so infuriated that she couldn't talk. She spun on her heel and rushed out of the office.

Quinn heard the warning bell. She was about to be late for her first riding class. She ran to her locker, grabbed her books, and slammed the door shut before taking off for the stables.

The smell of leather and horses filtered through the partition between the main stable and the girls' changing room. Quinn's heart was pounding, and her face was red. Having riding class at the same time as Cara and her friends was not her idea of fun after her confrontation with Mrs. Hartman. But there was nothing she could do about it, except keep her mouth shut.

She turned her back on the other girls, who were crammed into the small space to change into their riding clothes. Two sections of riders were changing at once. The Beginning Foals were beginners like Quinn and for some reason included Alicia Antona. Quinn thought she had been at Palm Beach Prep for years now and would be in a more advanced class. Kids like Stephanie were in Advanced Foals or Beginning Yearlings. Quinn couldn't remember which. She struggled into her brother's old cowboy boots and put her uniform blazer back on over her shirt. She still hadn't bought a riding jacket, and riding boots would have to wait. Before she knew that she'd be coming to Palm Beach Prep, Quinn had spent all her summer clothes money on a new really cool black leather bomber jacket just like her brother Sean's. It was Quinn's most prized possession. But now she had no more money to buy riding equipment.

"I heard Laura McChesney is having a boy-girl party next week at her house, and she's asking a ton of eighth-graders from G. Adams Prep," Patty Porter said loudly.

"And I haven't got a thing to wear!" Cara complained, her voice grating on Quinn's ears like fingernails on a chalkboard.

In the corner next to Quinn, Alicia let out a disgusted groan, loud enough for Quinn to hear.

Quinn cocked her head and studied Alicia. At least one other person in the room was clearly not a fan of Cara's. Not that Quinn cared. She reminded herself that as far as she was concerned, Cara Knowles simply did not exist. Who liked or disliked Cara was not Quinn's business.

"Did you ever find your watch?" asked a voice Quinn didn't recognize.

Quinn's whole body tightened. She could feel Cara looking in her direction. Cara's voice dropped down to a whisper.

An instant later, Cara's whisper gave way to a shriek.

"EEEEEEEEKKKKKKK!!!!"

Quinn spun around. Cara was hopping on one foot. The other foot was halfway into her riding boot, and she was kicking her leg wildly in the air.

"HELP!!!" she screeched again, and Jesse sprang up, yanked Cara's boot off, and gingerly put it on the floor.

"Don't touch it!" Cara screamed again, pushing Jesse away from the boot. For a moment, a circle of girls stared at the boot in dismay.

Cara looked up, and her furious glance settled on Quinn. "You did this! There's a—a"—Cara paused and shivered—"a—a snake or—a rat—or something in there. And you did it. You're going to be really sorry when I tell Heartburn about this!" Cara sputtered as she waved a finger in Quinn's direction. All the girls in the room turned accusingly toward Quinn.

"There's something in your boot?" Quinn said, still amazed. She walked over and picked up the boot and shook it. A bright-green lizard tumbled out. Shrieks filled the room. It landed squarely and stood still a second. Then it darted away through a gap where the barnboards met the ground.

"You put that there, Quinn," Cara declared as the riding instructor walked in. "You must have."

"What's going on in here, girls? Is someone hurt?" Candy Gordon asked as she looked around the room.

"Quinn stuck a lizard in Cara's boot!" Patty said instantly.

Quinn blew her bangs out of her eyes and didn't bother to deny the accusation. It was just too ridiculous.

"A lizard?" Miss Gordon looked from Quinn to Cara to the boot. She laughed and said, "Lizards, Cara dear, are everywhere. I found one in my briefcase the other day. And no one put it there. No one had to." Miss Gordon's voice was sweet but firm. Quinn breathed a sigh of relief.

The teacher checked her watch and frowned. "Come on, girls, you're late. The Stallions have already begun their round of jumps. Stephanie, get a move on. Foals and Yearlings, let's get out of here," she said, bending down and handing Cara her boot.

Cara shrank back in disgust, but under Miss Gordon's cool stare, she shook out the boot rather dramatically before putting it back on. Miss Gordon went to the door and waited for the girls to follow her out. Cara cast Quinn one final scathing glance and left the changing room flanked by her friends. While the girls paraded into the stable, Alicia turned and winked broadly at Quinn.

Quinn didn't have a chance to confront Alicia during class. All of her attention was focused on

Miss Gordon. Quinn had no idea that horses were so big. Miss Gordon wouldn't let them get on the horses, but instead demonstrated how to curry a horse, and explained all the equipment in the tack room.

After class, Quinn wondered if she was going to have to change her mind about Alicia. Anyone who had something to do with the lizard in Cara's boot couldn't be all that bad. She had to ask her, "Did you put that lizard—"

Alicia started laughing before she could even finish her sentence.

"Why'd you do that?" Quinn asked directly, cutting off Alicia's laughter.

"Well, Cara's been asking for it. I figured somebody had to do something."

"Thanks, Alicia," Quinn replied defensively, "but I don't need your help."

"It had nothing to do with you, Quinn. I'm just so sick of Cara Knowles. She's such a princess. But you have to admit I got her pretty mad. Wait till I tell Esme and Nicole about it," she said and giggled.

Quinn couldn't help but smile. Alicia's laughter was infectious. But it still didn't make sense to her. She didn't know what to think—but it was the first thing that had made her feel good since she'd gotten to Palm Beach Prep.

"Are you in a rush to get out of here? I was thinking that since I have to wait for Nicole, maybe we could sit in the bleachers and watch the Stallions' class for a while."

Quinn found herself saying "yes" before she had time to think about it. She couldn't put her finger on it, but there was something about Alicia that she really liked. So here she was, going to watch Nicole-the-Snob. Although maybe Nicole was O.K., since she and Alicia were such good friends.

Alicia led Quinn over to the bleachers by the riding ring, where Nicole's class was lining up to go over a series of jumps.

"Nicole's the best rider on the JV team. She's really good with horses," Alicia informed Quinn.

"So, why are you and Cara in my Foals class, then?" Quinn asked. "You've all been riding for so long."

"Well," Alicia explained with a laugh, "I don't exactly like horses. They kind of scare me, actually. And Cara totally hates them and puts down everything that has to do with them, from Miss Gordon to the ground they walk on. It makes me laugh, though, because her father makes her take private lessons so she'll get better. But nothing works."

"So, Miss Knowles-It-All is really not perfect at something," Quinn replied. "That's good to hear."

"Hey, watch Nicole—she's about to jump," Alicia exclaimed.

Quinn leaned forward and watched as Nicole, who looked so tiny on top of her huge bay horse, gathered herself before attempting to jump what looked to Quinn like an impossibly high barrier. As Nicole and her horse effortlessly cleared the jump, Quinn leaped to her feet, shouting, "Way to go, Nicole!"

"I told you she was great. I keep telling her she's going to make the Olympics," Alicia said proudly.

"So, how long have you and Nicole been friends?" Quinn asked.

"Ages. Since third grade when I started here. She and Esme have been friends since kindergarten. Nicole's a bit uptight with people, until you get to know her. She's incredible with animals, though. She wants to be a vet."

"Really?" Quinn asked. Maybe she had misjudged Nicole.

"But her family probably won't let her," Alicia continued. "They don't think being a vet is the right kind of job for a Whitcomb."

"Why not?"

"Well, they're very proper, and they don't think it would look right for a Whitcomb to be a vet. And then there's her father, but that's another story," Alicia replied vaguely.

Quinn thought Nicole sounded more and more interesting the more Alicia said about her.

"So, Quinn," Alicia said, interrupting her thoughts, "can you believe the big deal Cara's making over her stupid watch? It's so typical."

Quinn, immediately defensive, frowned at Alicia and retorted off the top of her head, "So *that's* why you wanted to talk to me? You just want to know if I took Cara's watch, like everybody else. Well, I didn't." She crossed her arms over her chest and stared hard at Alicia, her blue eyes boring into Alicia's warm brown ones.

"Quinn McNair, give me a break! All I did was ask you a question. I didn't accuse you of anything!" Alicia exclaimed, returning Quinn's stare.

Quinn looked down at her feet and scuffed her shoe against the cement. She knew her mother was right—she always jumped to conclusions. But still, it was so hard not to. "Alicia," she began, kicking a pebble with the toe of her boot, "I didn't mean to—I'm just so sick of all these people talking behind my back."

"Don't worry about it," Alicia replied reassuringly. "Cara has this way of driving people crazy. It's not just you."

"Well, it's hard because Heartburn seems to believe whatever Miss Knowles-It-All says."

"I know," Alicia agreed immediately. "She has this thing for Cara. It's disgusting."

"Well, they deserve each other, you know?"

"Yeah, really," Alicia agreed, and they both started to laugh.

Nicole walked over and sat down on the seat in front of them. "What's so funny?" she asked as she retied the blue ribbon around her ponytail.

"Nicole, you're such a great rider!" Quinn said excitedly instead of answering the question.

"Thanks. I love horses."

"So, are you ready to go?" Alicia asked as they got up to walk back to the changing rooms. "You're not going to believe what I did to Cara. . . ."

"What?" Nicole asked curiously.

Alicia was suddenly overwhelmed by a fit of giggles as she remembered Cara's scream. She couldn't talk for a moment, she was laughing so hard. And neither could Quinn. Nicole waited patiently. She was used to Alicia's giggle attacks.

"I put a lizard—" she choked out, laughing again.

"—in Cara's riding boot," Quinn continued. "You should have seen her face. She deserved it, though. She's such a snob. And I'm glad I told her so."

"You what?" Alicia and Nicole exclaimed in unison. "When?"

"At her party."

"You didn't!" Nicole exclaimed.

"In front of all her friends?" Alicia asked.

"Well, yeah," Quinn replied.

"No wonder she's out to get you," Alicia continued.

"Well, that wasn't the worst part. My friend Ricky works there sometimes because his dad's the gardener. So I was talking to him, and Cara got really mad. She told me I wasn't supposed to talk to the people who work for her. I don't know what the big deal was," Quinn said, shaking her head from side to side.

"I wish I could have seen her face," Nicole said, smiling at Quinn.

"Really," Alicia agreed as the three of them walked out of the changing room, down the drive, and out the gates of the school.

On her way home, Quinn shifted her knapsack up on her shoulder, and decided that Palm Beach Prep might not be so bad after all.

# CHAPTER 5

"Esme Farrell!" Nicole exclaimed as she swam with strong strokes over to her friend. "You haven't heard a word we said!" She, Alicia, and Esme were floating in the pool at the Targo Beach Club, one of Palm Beach's most posh resorts, and owned by Alicia's dad. Nicole glanced at the object of Esme's rapt attention and made a face. The boy, in Nicole's opinion, was really skinny and had funny knees. "Quinn's in all this trouble, and all you can think about is boys!" she exclaimed. Nicole thought boys were boring compared to horses anyway.

Alicia swam over to see what Nicole and Esme were arguing about. Nicole put a finger to her lips, and Alicia's eyes lit up. Alicia took one end of Esme's raft, Nicole the other, and they dumped her, soda glass in hand, right into the water.

After a loud splash and a gurgle, Esme came up

sputtering, her just-curled hair dripping wet. Nicole and Alicia quickly climbed the ladder and laughed their way to their lounge chairs, as Esme tried to wring the water out of her ruined curls.

"Some friends you are," Esme declared as she wrapped herself in the huge beach towel. She threw herself dramatically onto a nearby chaise lounge and put on her sunglasses.

"Sorry, Esme, but you were really asking for it. And the guy wasn't even that cute," Alicia apologized.

"Are you ready to listen now, Esme?" Nicole asked.

Esme threw on an oversized shirt that she'd tie-dyed herself, and propped her feet up on the table. "So, what were we talking about, anyway?" she asked, popping open a can of Coke.

"Esme!" Alicia said, completely exasperated. "What planet are you on?"

"Don't be mean," Nicole interrupted. "Esme can't help it. You know how she is."

"How am I?" Esme asked in a hurt tone of voice.

"You're fine," Alicia reassured her. "Back to Quinn. She's in a lot of trouble, and we've got to help her."

"Oh, you mean about the watch? But everybody thinks she took it," Esme stated.

"But *we* don't, Esme. That's the point," Nicole replied.

"We don't? Why not?"

"Because Nicole and I talked to Quinn after Foals, and she told us she didn't. She also told us what really happened at Cara's party," Alicia explained.

"You mean, when Quinn told Cara she made her sick? Well, that's not very nice," Esme said. "Cara didn't have to invite her in the first place."

"Well, Quinn only told her off after Cara made some obnoxious cracks about Nueva Beach," Alicia responded. "You know how Cara is. And you better believe she started the rumor that Quinn took her watch just to get back at her."

"Well, we're not absolutely positive, Alicia," Nicole interrupted in her practical way.

"But sure enough that we have to do something," Alicia continued. "And Cara can be such a weenie. It's so unfair to Quinn. What a terrible way to start a new school."

"I know," Nicole agreed. "I wish we could do something."

"Do we really have to worry about it right now?" Esme asked. "I was thinking maybe we could go to the mall."

"You're not going to believe this, but I've got the perfect plan," Nicole exclaimed suddenly. She fastened her brown eyes on Esme, who pressed herself back slightly in her chair. She had a feeling she wasn't going to like whatever plot Nicole was hatching.

"In the latest *Susie Parker and Pinto Pete* mystery—"

Alicia and Esme groaned in unison.

"No, listen," Nicole went on. "Pinto's been horse-napped just before the Belmont Stakes. Susie's friend, the teenage jockey wonder Linda Laroux, has a hunch that the new mystery black stallion is really Pinto cleverly disguised, but can't prove it. At Susie's suggestion, Linda infiltrates the notorious Markham gang, by pretending to be Bobby Markham's friend." Nicole looked eagerly from Alicia to Esme, then back to Alicia again. "See, it's perfect."

"*Loco!*" Alicia tapped her forehead.

"Definitely!" Esme agreed.

"Oh, I'm such an idiot, Nicole," Alicia yelled. "It's brilliant!" Alicia jumped up, pulling Esme up with her. "I don't think Esme got it, though."

"Got what?" Esme said as she freed herself from Alicia's grasp and backed up a few steps. Whatever Nicole and Alicia were cooking up, Esme had a feeling she was definitely not going to like it.

"Cara is secretly really jealous of you," Nicole said sweetly.

"So?" Esme asked, her eyes looking from Nicole to Alicia.

"You'll be like Linda Laroux in the story. You'll infiltrate!" Nicole announced.

"Infiltrate—you mean sneak in somewhere?" Esme asked as she scratched her head.

Alicia nodded solemnly. "Not somewhere— you'll become part of Cara's gang."

51

"Whaaat!" Esme squealed.

"Well, you *would* be perfect, Esme," Nicole went on excitedly. "You know Cara would jump at the chance to have you for a friend."

Esme kept shaking her head, but Alicia and Nicole went on and explained their plan.

"You'll hang out with them and then find out what really happened to Cara's watch," Alicia elaborated.

"You guys are crazed," Esme cried in dismay. "Cara hates my guts after that fashion show last year—"

"But that fashion show was last year," Alicia reminded Esme.

"Yeah, but Esme's right," Nicole said. "Cara looked like she was going to kill someone when not only did she not get to run it, but she didn't even get to wear the bridal gown for the grand finale."

"So that's that. There's no way I could possibly be her friend," Esme said, sounding hopeful. "Besides, she hates you two as much as she hates me. And she knows we're friends."

Nicole and Alicia weren't about to let her out of it so easily. "You could apologize to her," Alicia suggested.

"That probably wouldn't work," Nicole agreed with Esme. "Unless Cara thinks we're not friends anymore . . ."

"She's not that stupid, Nicole," Esme countered.

"But she'd secretly love to add a future *Seven-*

*teen* cover girl to her list of most important friends at Palm Beach Prep," Alicia pointed out. "So probably if you're nice to her—"

"And if we have a big fight right in front of her . . ." Nicole continued.

"She'll fall for it," Alicia concluded triumphantly.

"How can I fight with you guys?" Esme said in her most helpless voice.

"You're the one who wants to be an actress," Alicia replied. "This will give you the perfect chance to see how good you are."

"Well, I guess if it's a pretend fight that might be okay," Esme said, softening a little.

"But what'll we fight about?"

Nicole and Alicia answered at once, "Quinn!"

"But what'll Quinn think when we tell her about this?" Esme asked.

"We won't," Alicia answered immediately. "I'm sure she wouldn't want our help."

"Besides, she doesn't know Cara like we do," Nicole added.

"Anyway, it's about time somebody stood up to Cara the Creep," Alicia concluded.

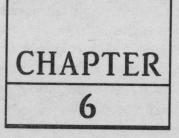

# CHAPTER

## 6

"Nicole Whitcomb!" Esme screamed over the noise in the hallway the next morning. Out of the corner of her eye, she saw several heads turn. "You've got to make a choice. It's me or Quinn!" she said in her most dramatic voice.

Nicole didn't bat an eye. "I don't know what you're talking about, Esme. I like Quinn. Besides, what right do you have to tell me who I can be friends with?" Nicole wondered if she had said the right line. They had rehearsed this little scene for hours the night before, but Nicole was nervous with so many people watching them.

"I, for one," Alicia said in a tone calculated to carry right to Patty The Mouth over by her locker, "don't think there's a choice, Esme. You are such an airhead, and I'm tired of hanging around with somebody who only talks about clothes."

Esme's eyes flickered with real hurt, and Alicia almost dropped out of character. "Esme?" she hissed between clenched teeth. "We're acting, remember?"

"You weren't supposed to say that, though," Esme countered as her eyes began to water.

Nicole noticed Jesse craning her neck in their direction. "Well, I've made my choice," she shouted as loudly as she dared. She knew there was supposed to be more to the argument, but she also knew Esme better than anyone. She could see that Esme had forgotten it was make-believe. Any minute, she would blow their cover. "You have no proof Quinn did anything wrong," Nicole continued.

Esme shook her head, trying to remember her lines. "I don't need proof. I don't need to wait around until something of mine is stolen."

Alicia winced as Quinn banged open the door of her locker. "If that's your final word, I've had it with you, Esme Farrell!" With that, Alicia marched right up to Quinn and steered her down the hall toward their homeroom.

"What was *that* about?" Quinn asked.

Nicole ran up behind them. "Phew!" she exclaimed. "That almost didn't work. Esme almost blew—" Then she remembered Quinn. "Uh, Quinn—"

Quinn looked past Nicole. "Wasn't Esme with you just now?"

55

"Forget about Esme," Alicia said, hiding her face in her notebook. "We just had a major fight."

Quinn stopped walking and blew her bangs off her forehead. "Hey, you were fighting about me, weren't you?"

"Well—" Alicia began.

"She's so dumb," Nicole interrupted, crossing her fingers inside her blazer pocket. She had never knowingly told a lie in her life—except to her mother about what she did at the stables Saturday mornings when she was supposed to be having extra jumping lessons. But Nicole didn't consider following the vet on his rounds a crime.

After school that day, Esme, Alicia, and Nicole stood on the corner of Worth Avenue. "Do I really have to do this?" Esme asked, ducking back around the corner of Worth Avenue. She looked first at Alicia, then Nicole.

Nicole shifted her gaze. "Es, we know it's hard, walking into Pizzarama and pretending to be Cara's friend—"

"*You* couldn't do it," Esme said, pouting.

Nicole's guilt mounted by several notches. "I couldn't. That's true."

"Of course, Nicole couldn't be a spy," Alicia added. "She can't act. Remember in third grade when she couldn't even act the part of a tomato in the 'Vegetables for Your Health' play?"

Nicole quickly backed her up. "And remember

how you were such a hit when you did my part, too, when I got so scared I ran off the stage?"

"That was nothing," Esme protested, basking in the compliment. "But that doesn't mean I'm a good enough actress to pull this off."

"You definitely convinced Quinn today," Nicole commented.

Esme smoothed down her kilt and checked her reflection in a store window one last time. Then she got on her bike and started around the corner. "Wish me luck!" she said over her shoulder, making a tragic face at her friends. As she rode the half-block to Palm Beach Prep's favorite after-school hangout, she experimented with various facial expressions. Parking her bike in the rack that fronted Worth Avenue, Esme settled on the perfect one—she'd look angry and hurt. After all, Nicole was Esme's very best and oldest friend. For the first time in eight years, Esme remembered how Nicole had rescued her at the kindergarten Christmas play by sharing her frankincense when Esme realized that she'd lost her myrrh somewhere between the auditorium and the parking lot.

Cara, Patty, Jesse, Stephanie, and Mimi were seated at the pizza parlor's best corner booth. "Hey, there she is now," Stephanie said, nudging Cara.

Cara eyed Esme. "So, you really think Esme's not friends with Nicole and Alicia anymore?"

"That was some fight they had this morning," Stephanie said, sounding impressed. "Nicole-Miss-Perfect-Whitcomb actually screamed at Esme."

"Hey, she's coming over here."

Esme eyed the one empty chair at the end of the booth. Then she smiled sweetly at Cara. "Can I sit with you guys?" she asked, looking away from them and down at the floor.

Cara thought about it for a minute, then motioned to the chair. "So, what's up, Esme?" Cara asked.

Esme tried to remember their plan. It would be too obvious to start talking about their fight right away. Esme looked at Cara with the saddest expression she could muster. "Not much," she replied, sighing deeply. "At least work's going all right. I'm doing some book covers for a new young adult series."

"Really!" the girls chorused in unison.

"Like the ones in the library?" Cara couldn't help asking.

Esme fluttered her eyelashes. "Yeah, the money's not bad, and my mother says it gives me exposure." She twirled a few strands of white-blond hair around her finger, trying to figure out what to say next. Suddenly, she remembered what Nicole had said about Cara just dying to have a cover girl for a friend. Esme's contract with *Seventeen* wasn't definite and had nothing to do with

58

the cover. It was only a shoot for a spring fashion spread, but still, she could lie just a little. "I may have something big coming up at *Seventeen*."

Cara fell for it immediately. "That's great!" she exclaimed, the other girls nodding in agreement.

"That must be so exciting," Jesse gushed.

"It's okay," Esme answered, shrugging her shoulders. "No big deal."

"And Alicia and Nicole are probably really jealous, right?" Cara asked directly.

"I guess so," Esme answered slowly, feeling terrible that she was lying so much. "But that's not the problem right now."

"Oh, your fight was about something else?" Cara probed.

"Sort of," Esme answered vaguely. "I guess I just finally realized what they're really like—"

"What do you mean?" Cara quizzed. "What are they really like?"

"Well, they'd rather be friends with a—delinquent—than be friends with me," Esme answered, proud of herself for having thought of such a big word. She shook her blond curls solemnly and scratched at a speck of peeling pink nail polish on the pinky of her left hand. When she looked up, her face was set in an angry frown.

"You mean Quinn?" Cara said eagerly.

Esme nodded violently. "Yes," she breathed. She poked out her bottom lip for effect and made it tremble. "I—I can't talk about it anymore," she said in a tiny voice as she buried her head in her arms, before her shoulders started to heave with silent laughter.

Cara looked at Esme's shaking shoulders in sympathy. The waiter came by bearing four slices of pizza and one Pizzamania Deluxe Pie with everything on it.

"Who ordered *that*?" Cara gasped.

Esme looked up. Her mouth watered at the sight of her favorite after-school snack. Just as her hand reached out to pull the pizza toward her, Cara turned to the waiter, and said with a sneer on her face, "There's been some mistake. Nobody here ordered a Deluxe. We wanted five slices." Cara glowed at Esme and added, "After all, we have a high-fashion model at our table. We could never eat stuff like that in front of her."

Esme watched in dismay as the waiter took her pizza away. It took every ounce of her not very strong willpower not to slide off the chair and grab it out of the waiter's hands. Esme pasted a martyred expression on her face and started eating her small, boring slice. She made a mental note to tell Alicia and Nicole that this spy routine couldn't go on for long, or she would starve to death.

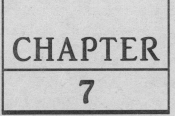

# CHAPTER 7

When the girls left Pizzarama, Cara walked Esme to her bike. "Hey, Esme, are you busy? We're going to go to my house and hang out by the pool. Do you want to come?"

Esme checked her watch. She had an hour before she was supposed to meet Alicia and Nicole at her house. "Sure," Esme replied as she followed the girls down Ocean Boulevard.

When they got to Cara's, they went up to her room and changed into their bathing suits. Esme was glad she happened to have a suit with her.

"Oh, wow!" Jesse exclaimed at the sight of Esme's lime-green-and-yellow-striped tank suit. "Where'd you get that? It's really cool."

"It's a sample for someone's spring line," Esme replied carelessly as she followed the girls down the stairs and outside to the pool. One of the bonuses of her modeling jobs was that her wardrobe was pretty well stocked with trendy clothes. Out of the corner of her eye, Esme could see the other girls admiring her. She hated to admit it, but she loved the attention.

"I wish the Swamp were co-ed," Patty said and sighed. She propped herself up on her elbows and peered over at Esme. "So, Esme, you must get to meet a lot of guys on your modeling jobs."

"Not really," Esme replied offhandedly before she remembered she was supposed to be getting on Cara's good side. "I haven't met a boy on a shoot in ages," she said. Then she giggled and swung her legs down from the chaise. "Mostly I've been working with other girls. My agent says I've been at an awkward stage."

All the girls, including Cara, gaped at Esme. "You? Awkward?"

Patty groaned and rubbed some suntan lotion on her slightly chubby legs. "I wonder what she'd say about me."

"You probably wouldn't want to know," Cara cut in obnoxiously and laughed. All the other girls, except Esme, followed suit.

"Still, it would be nice to meet some guys," Stephanie repeated.

"I bet Quinn knows plenty of guys—like your gardener, Cara," Jesse added in a snide tone.

"Quinn's definitely not pretty, though," Cara

said in a similar scoffing tone. She glanced toward Esme for confirmation.

Esme racked her brains for the least offensive thing she could say. "She *is* sort of tough-looking," Esme finally commented. Actually, Esme loved Quinn's red hair and blue-blue eyes.

"Tough," Stephanie snorted. "That's the understatement of the year."

"But I bet she gets to meet plenty of guys because she has an older brother. I think she said something about him being in a band," Cara said as she adjusted her pink sunglasses. "Not that I'd want anything to do with any guys from Nueva Beach, though."

"Really. I'm not even allowed to go there," Jesse added. "Meanwhile, you haven't gotten your watch back yet, right, Cara?"

"No," Cara replied sadly. "But what can you expect from someone like that? She grew up in a place where people probably think stealing is normal."

"So, you're positive she took it?" Esme asked.

"Of course," Cara said, shrugging off the question. "What else could have happened to it? If someone else had found it, she would have brought it to the office. Anyway, look at the way Quinn acted at my birthday party— Oh, you probably haven't heard about that, Esme."

Esme made a noncommittal noise and took a soda from a nearby ice bucket.

"She was incredibly rude!" Jesse exclaimed. "Really awful. She insulted Cara to her face at her own birthday party. . . ."

Cara leaned back in her chair as Jesse related the whole story, embellishing it quite a bit.

Esme tried to keep an open mind. Part of her couldn't believe that Quinn could be such an absolutely horrible person since Alicia and Nicole liked her so much. Still, it was Quinn's word against Cara's. Esme wasn't sure what to think. They made Quinn sound like a real jerk.

When Esme had to leave, Cara took her aside. "Listen," she said in a low voice, gesturing that she didn't want Jesse or the rest of her gang to hear. "I'm really glad you came today, and I wanted to apologize."

"Apologize?" Esme asked in surprise.

"About the fashion show last year. I was wrong. I thought I'd do a better job than you. But you were really good, Esme."

Esme blushed with pride.

"Really," Cara repeated.

Esme was stunned by Cara's praise. It was so unlike her to be nice.

"I was wondering whether you wanted to go to the mall tomorrow. I'd like to buy some new clothes, and the stuff my mother picks out on Worth Avenue just doesn't cut it." Cara took

Esme's arm and squeezed it chummily. "I'd like *you* to help me buy just the right clothes, since you're so good at it."

Esme's ego swelled. "Sure, Cara, that sounds like fun."

As Esme pedaled the last mile home, she started thinking. Cara had been so different . . . so nice. Perhaps, like Nicole, Cara had a secret side that she showed to people who knew her well. But then she reminded herself of the rotten things that Cara had done. She had dumped red dye in the pool before a big meet because Anne Marie Hayes, the swim team captain, had gotten more valentines from the G. Adams boys than Cara had. She had started a hate campaign against Nicole when Nicole had won a prize for best homemade molecule. Just this summer, she had declared all-out war on Alicia because Alicia was voted most popular during the school's annual beach party with G. Adams Prep. Just now, she had been mean to Patty about being a little overweight.

Esme didn't know what to think, but it definitely seemed like Cara was positive that Quinn had taken her watch.

Alicia and Nicole crossed the lawn in front of Esme's four-bedroom ranch house and rang the bell. Esme let them into the front hall. "Hi, guys," she said a little breathlessly.

"So, how'd it go? We staked out Pizzarama from

the minute you walked in!" Alicia exclaimed as Esme closed the door to her large and incredibly messy room. Alicia flung a pile of jeans and T-shirts off Esme's desk chair.

"I can't believe how quickly Cara fell for you."

"Yeah, we really fooled her," Nicole agreed. She hugged one of Esme's many lacy pillows to her chest.

"*I'm* the one who fooled her," Esme pointed out a little sharply as she scrambled into her favorite faded jeans with the holes over the knees.

"You're right," Nicole soothed. "After all, you did do all the work. And from what we saw, it looked like you did a great job!"

"So what happened?" Alicia asked excitedly. "You went to Cara's and . . ."

"Yeah. And we hung around the pool. We never actually got into the water, but we talked a lot."

"Yeah. . . ." Nicole prodded. "What'd you guys talk about?"

"Oh, clothes and stuff," Esme replied vaguely. "And lots about Quinn. They told me what she did at Cara's party. How she insulted Cara to her face and then left without even saying thank you. It totally didn't sound at all like the story Quinn told you, except for her telling them off."

"Of course not," Alicia exclaimed. "Cara always makes things sound the way she wants them to."

"So what did Cara say about the watch?" Nicole asked pointedly.

"Only that it had to have been Quinn who stole it because she couldn't imagine what else could have happened to it. She didn't say anything about making the story up to get Quinn in trouble." Esme shook her head slowly. "I don't know. Do you think . . . maybe . . . Quinn *did* take it?"

"What?" Alicia asked, flabbergasted. She jumped out of her chair and stood face-to-face with Esme. "Esme Farrell, how can you believe that creature-face, Cara Knowles? She always changes things around to make herself look good."

Esme slid dramatically down to the ground and started chewing on a piece of her hair. "I know, I know, but it's not like we really know Quinn either."

"Nicole and I talked to her, and it's obvious she's really upset about school. And she's really scared that she's going to get kicked out."

Esme looked confused. "She could be lying."

"No," Alicia said adamantly. "I always know when someone lies. The bottoms of their ears turn pink."

Esme and Nicole stared at Alicia. Then Nicole balled up one of Esme's pillows and threw it at her friend. "You can't be serious."

Alicia didn't even crack a smile. "That's what my mother always says. And she always knows when I'm lying."

"You're just weird," Esme replied, sighing. "I guess you're right, but still . . ."

Alicia and Nicole looked at each other. "What did Cara say to you anyway, Esme, now that you're suddenly taking her side?" Nicole asked.

"Nothing. She was pretty nice, actually."

"Give me a break!" Alicia screamed, throwing her hands up in frustration. "Of course she was. That's how she gets people to be her friends. Then she uses them, dummy."

"I know," Esme replied defensively. "I'm not that dumb, you know." She challenged Alicia and Nicole to disagree with her. "But you have no idea how hard it is to be a spy," she continued as she threw herself headlong across the bed.

"Well, you're doing great," Alicia exclaimed.

"So, when do you see her again?" Nicole asked.

"She said she wants to go shopping tomorrow—just the two of us, at the mall."

"The two of you?" Nicole speculated. "Then she really must like you."

"Don't make that face, Esme," Alicia said. "You love shopping no matter who you're with."

# CHAPTER
# 8

"**I** can't believe my mother never let me shop here," Cara exclaimed the next afternoon. She and Esme had been at the mall less than an hour, and already Cara had bought tons of stuff.

Esme found it hard to believe that anyone within a hundred miles of the West Palm Beach Mall could stay away from it. "Where did you say you buy your clothes?" Esme asked, steering Cara toward one of her favorite stores.

"Worth Avenue," Cara said, wrinkling her nose. "If you'd believe it. I mean the clothes are really well made, but they aren't fun like the stuff here. Anyway, with *my* allowance I can buy twice as much in a place like this. Can we go in here next?" Cara asked, sounding like a five-year-old kid let loose in a candy store.

Esme had never seen Miss Knowles-It-All look

so excited before. As she led Cara into the store, she couldn't help but admit that she was having fun. Cara was treating her as if she was some kind of fashion expert, and Esme definitely liked that.

Esme led Cara up to her favorite rack in the back of the store. "I modeled for this line last year," she casually mentioned. It wasn't like her to brag since she'd been modeling from the age of five and more or less took it for granted.

"Wow! I love this stuff!" Cara exclaimed. She flipped through the rack of shorts, miniskirts, and cute cropped tops. She picked out a pleated silver skirt and turned to Esme excitedly. "Look at this! I love it!" she said, holding it up in front of her.

*Oh, no*, Esme thought. *She's got to be kidding.* Cara, however, looked perfectly serious.

"Cara," Esme began gently. "I think the metallic look isn't for you. It's too flashy. You need something more . . . more subtle."

"Yeah, I guess you're right. So what color do you think is *me*?"

"Well, what about this?" Esme asked as she handed Cara a navy-blue-and-white-striped sleeveless minidress. "Why don't you try it on? I bet the blue would really bring out the blue in your eyes."

Cara smiled and walked toward the dressing room. Esme turned to look at herself in the three-way mirror. All of a sudden, Esme spotted movement to the left of her reflection. Then she heard giggling. She whipped around and found herself face-to-face with Alicia and Nicole. "What are *you* doing here?" Esme hissed.

"Esme, are you ready?" Cara called from inside the dressing room. "You're right. My eyes look so blue next to these stripes. You're a genius."

Cara opened the curtain and was about to step out and model her outfit when Esme grabbed the closest thing she could reach and shoved it into Cara's hands. "Cara, this is the real you," Esme sputtered and pulled the curtain closed.

"But this dress looks great on me," Cara insisted.

"It's okay, but it's so ... so ... common. And stripes are on their way out, you know."

"I guess you're right, but I don't know about *this*," Cara muttered as she slipped into the fuchsia and chartreuse polka-dot jumpsuit Esme had given her.

"Get out of here," Esme urged, practically pushing Nicole and Alicia away. Alicia was about to burst. Nicole clamped her hand over her mouth and dragged her behind a rack of cruise-wear.

Esme almost choked when Cara appeared in the chartreuse and fuchsia creation. "Cara, I have a good idea. Let's go have lunch now. I'm much too hungry to shop."

"So you don't think I should buy this, Esme?" Cara asked. "I thought you said it was me."

"Well, I changed my mind. Finding the right image takes time," Esme said. She pushed Cara back into the dressing room and closed the curtain.

Fifteen minutes later, hungrily eyeing the double cheeseburger at the table next to her, Esme stared sadly down into her small cup of frozen yogurt. Cara was so into the fact that all models had to diet that Esme was sure she'd starve to death before this spying business was over.

Esme heard familiar giggling behind her and turned around. A few tables away, she could see Nicole and Alicia peering around magazines they were holding up in front of their faces.

Esme gasped. "Cara," she began, interrupting Cara's story about her trip to France the summer before. "Let's switch seats. You'll get a better view of the mall from where I'm sitting."

"But I can see fine from where I am," Cara said as Esme pulled the chair out from under her. "I'm finished anyway. You want to just go?"

For the rest of the afternoon, Esme and Cara went into almost every store in the mall. On their way home, Cara started asking Esme all kinds of questions about modeling. It was fun talking to Cara about it. Nicole and Alicia were so used to it, they didn't get excited about it anymore.

"It must be really exciting modeling for all those catalogs and book covers," Cara began.

Esme nodded. "Sometimes it's lots of fun. Other times it's borrrring! Especially when the photographer makes you do the same shot over and over again."

"But you must get to meet some pretty interesting people on your shoots," Cara continued, anxious to show off her newfound grasp of fashion lingo.

"Yeah—some of the designers are really fun. But they're usually nervous wrecks on shoots," Esme said and giggled, telling Cara about the time when a young designer doing her first show was so crazed that she'd taken a tuck in a top and had pinned it to Esme's skin by mistake. It was fun for Esme to talk about modeling, but it wasn't helping her spying mission much. She tried to think of a way to turn the subject back to Quinn.

"So," Esme began. "Have you heard anything about your watch, Cara?"

"No, but I'm not surprised. Why would Quinn give it back?"

"I don't know, but are you sure she's the one who took it?" Esme asked, pleased that her spying was finally paying off.

"Of course I'm sure," Cara replied in her most Knowles-It-All way. "Hey, I have an idea. Do you want to have dinner at my house? We can rent a movie, and Dora can make popcorn."

"I can't," Esme replied. "I promised I'd be home early tonight. Maybe another time."

"Oh," Cara said, obviously disappointed.

"Maybe you could bring your portfolio over then. I'd love to see it."

"Okay," Esme agreed. She was proud of her portfolio and never had much of a chance to show it to the kids at school—except for Alicia and Nicole, and they were pretty bored with it by now.

When Esme got home early that evening, she went straight to her room and collapsed. Even though she was famished after the yogurt she'd had with Cara, she was too tired to move. She kicked off her shoes into the mound of clothes, books, and sneakers that covered the floor. Spying was even harder than school, Esme thought to herself as she drifted off to sleep. She was going to kill Alicia and Nicole.

# CHAPTER 9

"**Y**uck!" Quinn exclaimed as she wrapped the belt of her green and white polyester gym suit twice around her narrow waist. At least at Nueva Beach they'd gotten to wear their own shorts and T-shirts for gym. These outfits were gross, and they felt itchy and disgusting. She tugged on her sweat socks and tied her sneakers, then made her way through the narrow aisle of lockers.

She passed a group of girls she knew by sight from homeroom. Though they weren't in Cara's clique, as far as Quinn could tell, they fell silent as she walked by. Quinn felt the color rise to her cheeks. Obviously, word of the stolen watch had gotten around the school. Cara must have made sure that absolutely everyone believed she had taken it. Quinn looked up, her intense blue eyes burning with anger. Two girls nearby looked away.

For a moment, the silence in the locker room seemed incredibly loud. Quinn felt like screaming, but instead caught Cara's eye and stared her down until Cara started to smirk and had to look away.

When Quinn walked out into the gym, a short woman with red hair, like hers, approached. "You must be Quinn McNair. My name's Luellen Bosson, though most of the kids call me 'The Boss,'" she said with a smile. Quinn liked her immediately.

"We're doing relay races today, and as my old girls know, we generally begin with a light warm-up and a ten-minute run around the track. Do you run?" she asked, looking Quinn up and down. "You're built like a runner."

"No, but I was thinking of joining the middle school cross-country team. My brother runs track, and he's pretty good," Quinn replied, smiling at Ms. Bosson. Quinn loved people who were direct and said what they meant, unlike Heartburn, who never got right to the point.

After the class had run through their warm-ups, they gathered in the center of the gym. Ms. Bosson announced that they were to divide into two teams. "We're having relay races today, so let's pick our captains."

Her eyes lit on Stephanie. "Barnes, you head up the blue team."

"Dressed in these gross green gym suits, Ms. *Boss*on," Cara commented loud enough for everyone to hear. The way she accented the first syllable of Ms. Bosson's name and from the way the teacher's and Cara's eyes locked, Quinn realized that there was no love lost between these two.

Cara continued, oblivious to the way the Boss was staring at her. "I think we're old enough to wear track shorts and T-shirts like the seventh-graders. After all, we are in the middle school now."

"Way to go, Cara," Patty cheered from the back of the room, as several other voices shouted in agreement.

"The sweat rolls right off these gym suits, they're so polyester—yuck!" Jesse added, looking at Cara for approval.

"Really!" Mimi Roth echoed softly in a valiant attempt to show she was part of Cara's crowd.

"These are the pukiest things I've ever seen," Cara continued loudly.

Ms. Bosson's whistle shrilled. "Cara, for that little outburst, you will stay after class this afternoon and do ten extra laps."

"I will not!" Cara fumed.

"Oh, yes, you will!" Ms. Bosson boomed as Cara paled.

Another shrill blow on the whistle and the commotion died down. "As I was saying before I was so rudely interrupted, we are having relay races. Barnes heads the blue team, and . . ." Ms. Bosson searched the room.

"Quinn, you head the red team. It'll give you a chance to learn everyone's names."

Quinn's lightly freckled face reddened in surprise.

"All right, girls," the Boss continued as she proceeded to divide them into teams. "Farrell and Knowles on red," she began, peering at her roll book.

"Ms. Bosson," Cara interrupted loudly as all heads turned to look in her direction. "I absolutely cannot play on her team." She pointed at Quinn, with a look of total disgust on her face. "She's a thief and—"

"Cara Knowles!" Ms. Bosson and Quinn screamed at the same time. Ms. Bosson burst out, "You will shut that mouth of yours and go stand with the red team, or I will make sure you get detention for a week."

Quinn, meanwhile, had walked over to where Cara was standing and stood face-to-face with her, clenching and unclenching her fists. "You have no right," she sputtered, her blue eyes blazing fiercely, "no right at all to spread rumors about me behind my back. You're the biggest creep I think I've ever met, little Miss Knowles-It-All," she concluded before the Boss's whistle shrilled.

"Stop this at once, girls!" Ms. Bosson boomed. "You will do twenty-five sit-ups, and then we'll start the relays. Cara and Quinn, I want to see you both after class."

Cara glared at Quinn with daggers in her eyes as she lowered herself gingerly to the gym floor.

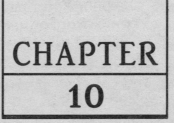

# CHAPTER
## 10

"Quiiiin," Alicia called, pedaling as hard as she could in order to catch up.

Quinn. slowed down a little when she realized Alicia was behind her. "Where are you off to?" Alicia asked, gasping for breath between words.

"Home," Quinn replied flatly.

"What's the matter?"

"You were in gym class. You know. I'm sick of Cara Knowles and her stupid games. I've had it with her and this whole school. Everyone thinks I took her stupid watch, and I just don't care anymore." Quinn started to pedal faster, dangling her arms by her sides and sitting up straight on the seat of her bike.

"Quinn, you can't give up. Cara's not worth it," Alicia said comfortingly as she struggled to keep up.

"I know, Alicia. But it's hard."

"Well, you're doing great, McNair. Really."

Quinn had to smile. Alicia was grinning at her, her black curls blowing wildly around her face. "Do you want to come over for a while?"

"Sure," Alicia replied, "I'd love to."

Soon they'd left Palm Beach behind and were whizzing down the commercial streets of Nueva Beach. Quinn turned left into a quiet residential area of small brick-faced, one- and two-story houses. Three short blocks later, she swung into a short drive. "This is it," she said, hopping off her bike and leaning it against the garage. "Come on in. Dad's truck's not here, and Mom won't be home from work for a while." Quinn explained that her father owned his own plumbing business and that her mother worked at a law firm in West Palm.

On their way up the steps, Quinn bent down quickly and removed a Tonka dump truck from the top step and tossed it into a sandbox. "Patrick, my little brother, is such a slob. He's always leaving his stuff everywhere."

As soon as the girls walked inside, their ears were assaulted by the sound of music. Someone was playing a catchy reggae rhythm on the drums, while a guitar struggled with the same riff again and again.

Alicia poked her head around the corner where the kitchen opened into a family room. A guy with

Quinn's straight auburn hair was bent over a guitar. A dark-haired Cuban boy was playing the drums. *"Buenos dias,"* the Cuban guy began when he spotted Alicia. At the sight of her Palm Beach Prep uniform, his face darkened, and he muttered something to the red-haired guy.

"Who are you?" the red-haired guy asked as Alicia found herself staring into dark blue eyes just like Quinn's. He sounded so hostile that Alicia gulped before answering. She shifted her gaze uncomfortably from his worn black hightops to his black T-shirt emblazoned with the words in bold red type: "Ziggy Marley—Conscious Party."

"Hi," Quinn said nonchalantly. She strolled into the room and handed Alicia a glass of juice. "Rick, Sean, I want you to meet my friend, Alicia." Quinn noticed Alicia's discomfort and then the anger on her brother's face. "You guys, Alicia really is a friend, one of the only two I've got at school. She's great."

Quinn's brother jumped up and put aside his guitar. He raked his hand through his hair in a gesture that reminded Alicia very strongly of Quinn. "Wow, sorry for the cold treatment. I'm Sean."

The Cuban boy pushed ahead of Sean and winked at Alicia. "And I'm Rick. I go to Nueva High and—"

"Hey, Guiterrez," Sean said as he playfully shoved Rick onto the couch. "Alicia is too young for you—and me, too." He snapped his fingers and made a disappointed face, then tousled Alicia's hair in a brotherly fashion. Alicia blushed.

"Hey, I really liked what you were playing when we walked in. Is it new?" Quinn asked Sean as she sat down cross-legged on the floor. Alicia plopped down beside her.

"We'll play for you," Rick bargained, "if you guys will dance. Then we'll know if what we're doing's any good."

"Especially since we're playing for the dance this weekend," Sean commented wryly. "Of course, you can't get the total effect without the whole band."

Then the music started, and Quinn jumped to her feet, pulling Alicia up with her. She moved with real rhythm to the strong reggae beat. "You're a great dancer," Alicia complimented her as they bopped wildly all over the floor. Rick cheered them on, and at the end of the song, Quinn and Alicia clapped.

"That was fun," Quinn said, flopping down on the couch.

"I'm really glad I came over," Alicia agreed, wiping the sweat off her forehead. "Nicole and Esme don't love to dance the way I do."

"Well, anytime you feel like it, there's always music over here," Quinn said with a smile.

\* \* \*

"Oh, Esme," Cara exclaimed as she sat on the edge of Esme's laundry-covered bed. "You are so lucky!" She closed Esme's portfolio and sighed.

Esme tried not to fidget. She had never been so nervous or upset in her entire life. Cara had been so awful to Quinn during the Boss's gym class. The worst part was, she couldn't believe that Cara had really biked home with her after that big scene. Especially since Esme had almost blown her cover when she actually giggled as Quinn had called Cara "Knowles-It-All."

"You know . . ." Cara began slowly, then stopped and bit her lip. She opened Esme's portfolio to a spread of a line of pre-teen sportswear. "You look different now."

"No makeup," Esme suggested. "I never wear makeup, except on a shoot."

"That's not it," Cara said as she swung her legs back and forth against the bed. "You look older now."

"Well, I hope *Seventeen* thinks so, too," Esme replied, looking at herself critically.

"They will," Cara said confidently. She closed the book and walked over to Esme's walk-in closet. The door was open, and Cara could see it was as messy as Esme's room. It was filled with tons of clothes. "I wish I did something of my own, like you do."

She turned to Esme, and for the third time that week, Esme had the feeling that she was seeing a side of Cara Knowles most people had never seen. "What do you mean, something of your own?" Esme asked, looking confused.

"You know, like you're a model, Stephanie's a jock."

"*You*'d like to be a jock?" Esme had to laugh as she eyed prissy Cara, who hated to work up a sweat more than anything in the world.

"Don't laugh at me, Esme," Cara said in a hurt voice. "I mean it. I wish I did something special. Maybe if I was talented like you or good at art or something, my parents would be around more." Cara's voice suddenly sounded very small.

Esme couldn't believe what she was hearing. Cara Knowles, the bully, was actually on the verge of tears. Poor Cara, Esme thought. Suddenly, Esme was absolutely, completely, and totally overwhelmed with guilt. Cara was confiding in her what she probably hadn't told anyone else in the world—except maybe Jesse, who'd been her best friend for as long as Esme could remember. And Esme was no friend at all. She was worse than no friend. She wasn't even an enemy—she was a spy!

"Cara," Esme began before she could stop herself, "there's something I have to tell you. . . . I'm not—" Suddenly, the phone rang.

"Hi," Esme shouted with relief into the receiver.

"Es?" Alicia asked, rubbing her ear gingerly at the other end. "Are you all right?"

"Uh, sure," Esme said, repeating silently to herself, "I must not say her name, I must not say her name," half-relieved and half-sorry she hadn't told Cara the truth.

"Cara's there," Alicia finally realized. "With you, now."

"You can say that again!" Esme said and laughed. She wanted Cara to think she was talking to a friend, which, of course, she was, though it was someone who Cara thought was no longer her friend. Esme rubbed her temples. All this spying was giving her a headache.

"Listen, Es, you have to find out some major information. Poor Quinn's going crazy."

"How am I supposed to do that?" Esme squeaked.

"Twenty-five cents for the next three minutes, please," the operator interrupted. Esme heard coins clanking and then Alicia was back on the line.

"Esme, are you still there?" she asked.

"Yeah," Esme answered. "Hang on a second." Esme turned to Cara, who was holding one of Esme's sweaters up in front of her as she stared into the full-length mirror on the back of the closet door. "That color would look great on you, Cara. Why don't you try it on?"

Cara didn't need to be urged. "You have the

coolest clothes, Esme," she said as she slipped the sweater over her head. She admired herself for a moment and then dove back into Esme's walk-in closet. Esme could hear her mumbling, "I've never seen so many shoes."

Esme went back to Alicia. "I'm back," she whispered.

"Es, I just left Quinn's," Alicia continued. "She's really upset about what happened in gym. We really have to prove that Cara's lying."

"You just said that," Esme complained.

"I know. But it's really important. It's all up to you, Esme."

"But I don't know what else to do!" Esme whined, glancing over her shoulder toward her closet.

The operator cut in again. "Twenty-five cents, please." There were no coins clanking this time, though, and Esme could barely hear Alicia mumble something about no change. Then the line went dead. Esme stared at the dead receiver for a moment before replacing it. She turned reluctantly back to Cara. Esme had had it with spying.

# CHAPTER 11

"Warning," Mrs. Hartman intoned late the next morning, "means that one more incident will force me to put you on probation." She looked hard into Quinn's blue eyes. "Have I made myself perfectly clear?"

"Yes," Quinn replied. She felt as if the walls were closing in on her. And she had serious doubts about her ability to act the part of Miss Perfect Palm Beach Preppie.

"And do you understand why your behavior warrants a warning?"

"I think so," Quinn said, her voice low. "Because of Cara and the fight the other day." She looked up quickly to meet Mrs. Hartman's icy gaze.

Mrs. Hartman frowned. "The point is we can't have someone with an uncontrollable temper disrupting this school. The girls of Palm Beach Prep know how to behave with decorum, and you should follow their example."

Quinn could have told Heartburn a few things about her precious Palm Beach Prep girls. It was all she could do to hold her tongue.

"As for the watch—" Mrs. Hartman said with a sigh as she studied her large gold wedding band.

"I didn't take it, you know," Quinn interrupted.

"I would like to believe you had nothing to do with the missing watch. And there is no evidence you took it. So I think we will all do our best to forget about it."

Quinn wanted to feel relieved, but she couldn't. She hadn't stolen the watch to begin with, and she had a funny feeling that unless the mystery of the watch was solved, the next time someone lost something, she would be blamed all over again.

By the time she left Mrs. Hartman, first-shift lunch had begun. Quinn avoided the crowd pouring into the cafeteria and walked down the short corridor to the library.

Even though the temperature was hot, the room was cool. Quinn bypassed the low shelves and small round tables of the children's section and sought refuge in the stacks. She wandered down a row marked "Fiction, A–E," trailing a finger along the spines of the books. Quinn sighed heavily. She vowed that no matter how bad things got at PBP, she'd stick it out to the end. She had worked so hard for her scholarship, and she wasn't about to give up now.

"Quinn McNair?" Mr. Holmes's voice made Quinn jump.

He was standing at one end of the aisle, holding a copy of *Huckleberry Finn*, the book he'd assigned to Quinn's class.

"Shouldn't you be at lunch?"

"Is having lunch in the cafeteria a rule?" she asked, alarmed. Not even twenty minutes had passed since she'd spoken to Mrs. Hartman, and she'd already done something wrong.

"Rule?" Mr. Holmes asked, puzzled. "About eating lunch?" He laughed. "Not at all. You can do whatever you want to during lunch period, except leave school grounds."

"Oh, good," Quinn exclaimed with enormous relief.

At Mr. Holmes's next words, she got nervous again. "I'm glad I caught you here. I've been meaning to talk to you, Quinn."

Quinn paled slightly. She had half forgotten that Mr. Holmes wasn't just her English teacher. He was also the assistant principal. He probably knew everything—about Cara, the watch, the fight, her warning.

"How do you like PBP so far?" he asked conversationally.

Quinn didn't know what to say. She averted her

gaze from his face, looked around the room, and then down at her hands. "Okay," she said at last.

"It's hard fitting in at a new school," he replied sympathetically, his beautiful brown eyes looking with concern at Quinn. She could understand why every girl at PBP had a crush on him. He brought new meaning to the words tall, dark, and handsome.

"Fitting in?" Quinn echoed. "You think I'm having trouble fitting in?"

"Well, you've been looking a little bit down. And I think you've been working too hard—studying too much—trying to live up to your scholarship. You should do other things besides study. PBP has a lot to offer. So what clubs have you looked into joining?"

Quinn wondered if she'd even be at PBP next week the way things were going. "I haven't really thought about it."

"What about the paper? I know you love to write."

"I don't think so, Mr. Holmes," Quinn said a little stiffly, more than sure that Cara would never let her near the paper now.

He looked a little surprised but shrugged. "How about Checkmates? That's our competitive chess team. Or the physics club, or the debating team?"

Quinn grimaced. Mr. Holmes must have thought she was a real nerd.

"Well, actually, I was thinking of joining the cross-country team," Quinn replied.

Mr. Holmes looked a little taken aback. "Did you know that I'm the coach?"

Quinn shook her head and smiled. Things might not be so bad after all, she thought.

The bell rang, signaling the end of the lunch period. "See you in English, Mr. Holmes," Quinn said as she slung her knapsack over her shoulder and left the library.

# CHAPTER 12

Cara Knowles was on the verge of hating her father. Ninety-nine times out of a hundred she could wrap him around her little finger, but he had one blind spot where she was concerned. He was determined that she would become a championship horseback rider. He wanted Cara, not Nicole Whitcomb, to be captain of the junior equestrian team. And Cara positively, absolutely, and totally hated horses. Even the smell of them made her sick. More to the point, Cara thought as she stomped away from her riding class, horses hated her.

Still wearing her jodphurs, Cara grabbed her bag from the stable changing room and headed across campus to get her books from her locker. She had invited Jesse, Stephanie, Patty, and Mimi to her house for a cookout on the beach. They were supposed to meet her by her locker.

She banged down the row of gray metal lockers toward her own. Jesse was waiting in front of her locker. Stephanie and the others were hanging out by the vending machines at the end of the hall. "Hi, Cara," Jesse greeted her, then noting the dust on the back of Cara's pants, cut herself short. "Uh—you—"

"I know, I fell again," Cara snapped. "That dumb horse. I hate her."

"I know you do," Jesse said and slid down to the floor, waiting for Cara to get her things together. Whenever she was upset, Cara took forever to get out of school. Jesse yawned and buried her head on her arms and settled in for a long wait.

Cara opened her locker and pulled out her books. She started stuffing them into her gym bag. "There's so much junk in here."

"Hmmmm," Jesse murmured without looking up.

Cara began dumping her sweat pants, gym suit, towel, and sneakers onto the floor. "All this stuff. I have to get a bigger bag." Cara shook out her gym suit, and noticed something bright snagged on the belt. She shook it again and something clunked down on the floor. Cara frowned and bent to pick it up.

*My watch!* she thought. So her watch had been in her bag all along. She started to smile and turned to Jesse. She was about to tell Jesse but then clamped her mouth shut. What would people think if they found out she'd had her watch in her gym bag all along? They'd realize it hadn't even been stolen and that Quinn McNair wasn't really a delinquent. Heartburn would kill her.

Cara held her breath and looked at Jesse. Jesse's head was still resting on her arms. She hadn't seen a thing. Hastily, Cara jammed the watch back into the bottom of her bag. She stuffed the rest of her clothes into the locker and then jumped up. "C'mon, Jess, let's get out of here."

As they headed toward the bike rack, Cara's mind was in a whirl. Should she confide in Jesse? Cara suddenly wondered if she could really trust her. What if Jesse accidentally mentioned it to The Mouth? It would be all over school in exactly three minutes flat. Everyone would laugh their heads off. Cara envisioned Alicia and Nicole's reaction to the news. Cara would die before she became a laughingstock. And then there was Quinn. At the thought of Quinn, Cara paled. Looking like a jerk would be the least of Cara's worries if the truth about the watch ever came out. Heartburn was all over Quinn for something she hadn't even done. For a full ten seconds, Cara felt totally guilty—until she remembered how Quinn had insulted and humiliated her in front of her friends. Cara tried to envision spending the next couple of years of her life in the company of Quinn McNair. Quinn, who had that disgusting way of always becoming the center of attention. Cara pressed her lips together and tightened her grip on her bag. No one was ever going to find that watch.

# CHAPTER
## 13

At the sound of the last bell on Friday afternoon, the halls of Palm Beach Prep were swarming with girls yelling and banging their lockers in anticipation of the weekend. Esme ducked into the bathroom, praying that she wouldn't see Cara. That morning she had left notes in Alicia and Nicole's lockers telling them to meet her at the stables at exactly three-fifteen. She checked her watch. She had only four minutes to get there, and she had to make sure she didn't run into any of Cara's clique on the long walk to the stables.

She pulled her sunglasses out of her knapsack and put them on. Spies in movies always disguised themselves with sunglasses. She opened the bathroom door and scooted around the corner. She stopped short so she wouldn't bump into the retreating backs of Mimi and Stephanie. She looked around wildly. She bent over and tried to lose herself in the crowd of girls leaving the school.

As she scurried along the hallway, Esme vowed she'd never be a spy again. It involved too much exercise. She ran down the steps and along the path leading to the stables. A light rain was falling, and the ground was slippery. She had to be careful not to slide in the mud. Gasping for breath, Esme reached the stables and flung open the door. It was so dark in here. She'd never be able to find Nicole and Alicia.

"Nicole? Alicia?" she hissed into the darkness. A horse snorted, and Esme jumped.

"Es?" Alicia asked warily. "Is that you?"

"Did anyone see you?" Nicole asked as she stepped out of one of the empty stalls.

"I can't see you guys. Where are you?"

"You're so silly, Esme. Why are you wearing sunglasses? It's raining," Nicole admonished.

"I had to make sure no one would recognize me," Esme said proudly as she removed her sunglasses. "Wow, I can see you. No wonder it was so dark."

Alicia shook her head. Esme was such a space cadet. "So, why'd you want to see us? Did you find out about the watch?" Alicia asked excitedly.

"No—" Esme began, then stopped.

"So what is it?" Nicole asked in confusion. Nicole looked more closely at Esme's face and stopped talking. Esme's jaw was jutting out in a way Nicole knew all too well. Esme didn't get stubborn about things very often, but when she did . . . "What's up, Esme?" she asked again.

Alicia shook her head in disbelief. "You didn't find out about the watch? Then why blow your cover and meet us here?"

"Because there isn't going to be any more cover to blow!" Esme said firmly. "I won't spy anymore. Ever. For Quinn or for anyone."

"What's with you?" Alicia exclaimed, throwing up her hands and marching right over to Esme. "Are you kidding? Quinn's still in trouble, and she's counting on us—"

"She doesn't even know about us," Esme interrupted. "She thinks I hate her."

"I'm sure she doesn't think that," Nicole added.

"But what made you change your mind now? Was it Cara? Don't tell me you actually believe she wants to be your friend, Esme!" Alicia said with scorn in her voice.

Esme tossed her thick french braid back from her shoulder and said with dignity, "I think she does. In fact, I know she thinks I'm one of her very best friends. Not that I am her friend. And I don't want to be, either. I'm not that stupid," she reminded Alicia.

"No one said you were stupid, Es," Nicole soothed, "but I don't understand what happened."

Esme's voice quavered dangerously. "Cara thinks I'm her friend, and she's telling me things she wouldn't tell anyone. She trusts me. And that makes me feel terrible. I don't like Cara Knowles. And she isn't my friend. I wish I never had to see her again. But I will not spy on her. Not anymore. It's wrong." Esme's chin jutted out a little further.

"This is ridiculous," Alicia fumed.

"No it's not," Esme maintained.

Nicole was silent. "Esme has a right not to spy anymore. I wouldn't want to do it. If Esme wants to stop, then she should."

Esme gave Nicole a grateful look. "So you understand? I just can't lie like that. It's wrong."

"What's wrong is letting Quinn take the blame for something she didn't do," Alicia said hotly. "I don't know what's gotten into you. Really I don't. Now I have no idea what we're going to do."

Esme shifted uncomfortably, and Nicole came to her rescue. "What we're going to do is go to my house and make chocolate chip cookies."

Alicia scowled, but Esme didn't see. "I'll meet you there in half an hour," Esme said, knowing Alicia wasn't one to hold a grudge for long. "I didn't bring my bike today, so I've got to grab the bus."

Esme took a shortcut through the hockey field. As she burst through the bushes near the bus stop, fishing in her knapsack for her bus pass, a horn honked once and then a second time. At the third honk, she looked up. A long black limousine had pulled up to the curb. Cara poked her head out the back window.

"Esme, where have you been? I've been looking for you all over," Cara scolded playfully. "Hop in. I have a surprise."

"I can't," Esme squeaked. "I've got—"

"Oh, come on. It's Friday. Whatever you've got to do can wait. You have to come to my house."

"James," Cara instructed the chauffeur, "open the door for my friend."

Esme looked around in a panic, trying to think of a way out. Going to Cara's house was the last thing on earth she wanted to do, but she couldn't come up with an excuse quickly enough, and a moment later, she found herself in the back seat, listening to Cara describe her latest shopping spree.

"I bought us something special," Cara said as the limo pulled into her driveway.

"What'd you buy?" Esme asked, trying to sound as enthusiastic as Cara looked.

"This special French earth face masque," Cara said proudly.

"A what?"

"The lady at the store said that it revitalizes tired skin cells. But you probably know all about that, since you're a model."

Esme didn't know the first thing about masques, but she decided it would be easier to do what Cara

100

wanted, so she could leave as soon as possible. She followed Cara into her room.

A little while later, Esme heard herself saying, "Now, the secret to a good masque is to lie down and relax." Esme eyed the bowl of mud and wondered why French dirt was better than the American kind. She rattled on to Cara, making up instructions as she went along. Actually, slopping mud all over Cara's face might be kind of fun. If only Alicia and Nicole could see her now, Esme thought. "You can't talk, or smile, or even move while it dries," Esme instructed. She wasn't sure about the moving part, but it sounded sort of right.

"I don't see why we can't do this by the pool," Cara complained as Esme slopped a fistful of brownish-green goo onto her face.

Esme had no idea why either, but thought quickly. "Because the sun will dry the masque too fast. You don't want to get wrinkles," she said in what she thought was a very professional tone.

"Nooo!" Cara said, horrified.

When she was finished, she studied the effect of Cara's face covered in mud. She had to smile. Then she realized Cara was watching her.

"Don't laugh at me," Cara mumbled through clenched teeth, trying not to move her mouth.

"Don't talk or the masque will crack," Esme reprimanded ominously.

"Now, for your eyes." Esme knew she had to

cover Cara's eyes. She didn't want Cara watching her. She didn't want to be Cara's friend. She didn't want to be a spy anymore, either. She couldn't cover her eyes with clay, but she remembered one of the other models putting cucumber slices on her eyes to get rid of wrinkles.

"I'll be right back," she said, warning Cara not to budge. She dashed down to the kitchen, cornered Dora, then a moment later was up again. She put the cucumber slices over Cara's eyes. "Now, this is something models do all the time. It takes away the bags under their eyes. Not that you have bags under your eyes, Cara, but it will keep you from getting any," Esme improvised.

"Pmmm onnn smmm msssic!" Cara commanded through clenched teeth.

Esme stared blankly before she finally translated Cara's mumble. "Music." She clapped her hands. "Great idea!" She set a timer for ten minutes, then studied Cara's collection of disks and popped her favorite Debbie Gibson disk into the CD player. She turned up the sound really loud so she wouldn't have to talk to Cara.

Then she dropped down onto the chair in front of Cara's vanity and sighed. How do I ever get myself into such messes? Esme thought. She would much rather be making cookies with Alicia and Nicole. Esme propped her chin on her hand and began to examine the objects on the table. She noticed a really pretty porcelain box in the shape of a heart. She knew she shouldn't open it, but she couldn't help herself. Biting her lip, Esme peeked at Cara's reflection in the mirror. Cara's cucumbers were still in place, her mouth set in a firm narrow line. With one eye still on Cara, Esme quietly pried off the top of the box. Inside, she saw something plastic and neon-colored. Esme toyed with it a moment, then her blue eyes opened very wide. It was Cara's watch! So Cara hadn't lost her watch at all. It was on her vanity, in this box, all along. She must know she had it. How could she accuse Quinn?

Esme panicked. She stuffed the watch in her blazer pocket and started for the door. Just at that moment, the music stopped—the timer buzzed— and Cara took the cucumber slices off her eyes.

"Hey, where are you going?"

"Home. I mean—" Esme sputtered. "I have a booking—I forgot. I'll see you later."

"My masque!" Cara screamed in horror, touching the caked mud on her face.

"Wash it off—read the instructions," Esme called over her shoulder as she tore down the hallway and down the stairs. The watch seemed very heavy in her pocket.

When Esme reached the Whitcomb estate, she pushed the door open without even knocking and flew straight to the kitchen at the back of the house.

"Nicole, Alicia!" Esme burst into the room, gasping.

The two girls looked up from the pile of cookies they were putting into a jar. "Where have you been?" Nicole demanded.

"Look! Look!" Esme couldn't catch her breath to say more. She fished in her pocket and pulled out the watch. She waved it in the air.

"What's that?" Alicia exclaimed, wrinkling her nose in distaste.

"Tacky!" Nicole quipped.

"Beyond plastic!" Alicia tittered.

"Totally neon!" Nicole added.

Esme couldn't believe that they didn't realize what this was. "You guys! This is Cara's watch. I took it."

Alicia leaped to her feet. "Cara's watch?"

"Where'd you get it, Esme?" Nicole asked curiously.

"Quinn never took it. Cara had it the whole time," Esme explained.

Nicole got up and took the watch from Esme. "But how did you get it?"

"I found it on Cara's vanity."

"Where?" Alicia gasped.

"When?" Nicole asked.

"Just now—"

"You were at Cara's?" Alicia exclaimed as she shook Esme by the shoulders. "I do not understand you. One minute you will never talk to

Knowles-It-All ever again, and the next minute you're at her house. Esme, I can't keep up with you."

"But I found the watch, didn't I?" Esme replied, wondering why they weren't more excited. She grabbed a cookie and dropped into a chair at the kitchen table. She smiled happily at Nicole and Alicia, feeling more than proud of herself.

Nicole frowned and said, "Esme, what have you done?"

"What do you mean? I found the watch," Esme repeated.

"And what are we going to do with it?" Nicole asked, tapping her foot noisily against the polished floor.

Esme slowly shook her head. "I don't know."

"What should we do with it?" Alicia was as puzzled as Esme. She sank down in a chair next to Esme. "We found the watch. We just have to bring it to Heartburn on Monday," she told Nicole.

"And where do we tell her we found it?"

"We tell Heartburn the truth," Esme replied. It was perfectly clear to her.

"That won't work. Heartburn will just talk to Cara, and Cara will lie. She'll say we got the watch from Quinn because we're her friends."

"Let's think this out," Alicia suggested. "We've got to prove that Quinn never took that watch. Now we know Cara had it at home. Telling Heartburn won't help, but—" Alicia's eyes began to sparkle.

"I feel a plan coming on," Nicole said. She crossed the room and sat down on the other side of the table.

"I've got it!" Alicia announced triumphantly as she reached for another chocolate chip cookie.

# CHAPTER

## 14

"Why are we sitting here?" Quinn grumbled. It was Monday and raining, and the cafeteria was jammed: Alicia and Nicole had plopped themselves down at a table right behind Cara. Quinn eyed her from the back and promised herself that she would not under any circumstances be pushed into another fight. Just now, in the cafeteria line, Heartburn had actually smiled at her. Quinn was almost beginning to hope that she might be off "warning" soon.

Alicia didn't answer Quinn right away. She stuck a straw in her container of milk. Only then did she look up at Quinn. "Sitting here won't hurt—not for one day," she said as she grinned at Quinn. Quinn got the distinct feeling that Alicia was up to something, but she had no idea what.

Nicole, on the other hand, looked very nervous.

She kept picking up her apple, then putting it down again, and smoothing her napkin with her hand. She seemed about to say something.

A moment later, Esme marched by their table, her nose in the air and her hair in a high ponytail that matched Cara's. She sat down beside Cara. Quinn couldn't get over how much they were beginning to look like twins.

"Sitting next to Knowles-It-All is not a good idea," Quinn whispered to Nicole.

"Don't worry," Nicole replied and gulped loudly.

At the next table, Cara elbowed Jesse. "Look who we've got for company!"

"It's enough to make you throw up to have to eat with people like that," Jesse remarked and dramatically turned her back on Quinn.

"I thought Quinn was getting expelled or something," said The Mouth loudly.

Esme took a bite of her tuna casserole then bent over in her chair.

"Hey, are you okay?" Cara asked, watching Esme suddenly duck under the table.

"Uh, yeah—dropped something . . ." came Esme's muffled reply. Esme groped under the table for Cara's bag. She was having a hard time telling the difference between bags, knapsacks, and legs.

"Hey, what's going on under there?" Stephanie

shouted. Esme poked her head up. "Uh—I can't find something in my purse," Esme lied.

"That was my foot, stupid!" Stephanie growled, but Esme just grinned dumbly at her.

"Sorry," Esme said as she vanished under the table again.

At the next table, Alicia grabbed Quinn's arm and pinched it hard. "Pray," she mouthed to Nicole.

"What's going on here?" Quinn's gravelly voice boomed.

"Shhhhhhh!" Nicole clapped her hand over Quinn's mouth.

"You'll ruin everything," Alicia hissed.

Quinn followed Alicia's glance to Cara's table. "Don't look!" Nicole warned in a loud whisper.

"Hey, Cara, remember that hair clip I lent you last week?" Esme asked as she emerged from under the table.

"What hair clip?" Cara replied, looking blankly at Esme.

"You know, when we were at the mall, and you wanted to put your hair up and I gave you the blue one I was wearing," Esme explained patiently. "The bluey-purple one I said matched your eyes."

"Right . . ." Cara remembered vaguely, basking in the compliment.

"I wanted to wear it tonight. I'm—uh—going out with my dad, and he gave it to me, so . . ."

Esme sank down a little in her seat. Lying wasn't as easy as it was cracked up to be.

"I don't think I have it with me," Cara said, toying with her ponytail.

"But you put it in your bag. I saw it!" Esme said desperately.

"I'm positive it's not there, Es."

"It must be," Esme said as she yanked the bag out from under the table. "I saw you put it in there."

Before Cara could say anything else, Esme turned the bag upside down and dumped the contents on the table.

Nicole got up, and so did Alicia. They pulled Quinn to her feet. "Hey! What?" she exclaimed before Alicia clapped her hand over Quinn's mouth.

Cara stared at the mess on the table. Then her eyes widened in shock. "How did my watch get here?" she shrieked. "I left it at home—" When she realized what she had said, she blushed furiously.

"Your watch!" Quinn exclaimed loudly, making heads turn across the cafeteria. "You've had your watch all along. You sneak. You liar. You—"

It was Jesse who leaped to Cara's defense. "Why'd you stand up, Quinn? You must have known what was in the bag, didn't you? You put it there, Quinn McNair, just to get Cara in trouble."

"How could she put it there?" Mimi asked. "Quinn hasn't been near Cara for ages, and she sure hasn't been at her house since the watch was stolen—"

Cara glared at Quinn. "She must have done it. She must have sneaked into my house and put it there when no one was looking."

Stephanie burst out laughing. "That's crazy, Cara. Why would Quinn do a thing like that? Besides, your dad has a pretty major security system. Remember the time we tried to sneak out to the beach during a slumber party? I've never heard so many alarms ringing."

"Maybe you never wore it to school that day," Jesse suggested, not sure what to think.

"I wore it to school. And Quinn stole it. And I don't know how it got in my bag." Cara looked around at her circle of friends, frantic for some sign of support. Stephanie, Jesse, Mimi, Patty, everyone at the table looked as if they didn't believe her.

"I do," Esme said, and the table fell silent. "I know how it got in your bag. I put it there. I found it in a box on your vanity on Friday night, and I put it in your bag just now. I wanted everyone to see you'd had it all along."

"You!" Cara exclaimed, staring at Esme. Slowly, the truth hit her. "You've been Quinn's friend all along?"

"She has?" Quinn whipped around and looked

111

at Alicia and Nicole. From the way they were grinning, Quinn knew that what Cara said was true.

"I sure have, Cara Knowles," said Esme defiantly. "I was trying to find out what happened to the watch."

"You—you planted it in my house. Quinn gave it to you." Cara turned to the crowd gathered around the table. "See, Quinn stole it after all." Cara looked triumphantly first at Quinn, then at Alicia and Nicole, and finally, at her friends. It was obvious that no one believed her. Slowly, Cara's cheeks began to burn. She spotted Esme's half-eaten tuna casserole. Suddenly, she picked it up and dumped it right on Esme's head.

"Ooooooohhhh!" Esme screeched.

"FOOD FIGHT!" Alicia hollered, and hurled the remains of her green jello in Cara's direction. It landed right in Jesse's lap.

Next, Quinn grabbed Nicole's cottage cheese and marched right up to Cara, and threw a fistful in her face.

Food was flying everywhere.

"WHAT IS GOING ON HERE?" Mrs. Hartman boomed. A meatball whizzed dangerously close to her head. Then the room fell silent.

Mrs. Hartman ignored everyone but Quinn. "I knew you'd be at the center of this," she announced grimly.

"Cara started it!" everyone said at once.

Mrs. Hartman had to turn around. She gasped. Cara's uniform was plastered with cottage cheese, tuna fish, and noodles. "Get a napkin, Cara, and clean yourself off." Then she noticed the watch lying in the middle of the table. "Why, Cara, you found your watch? Why didn't you tell me?"

"Because I—I—" Cara sputtered.

"She didn't have a chance yet, Mrs. Hartman," Jesse explained, coming to her rescue. "It must have been stuck in her bag, in a compartment or something, and when Esme dumped the stuff on the table, it fell out."

"Is that true, Cara?"

Cara looked down at her shoes. When she looked up again, her eyes locked with Quinn's. "Sort of," she finally admitted.

"I told you to check your things carefully, didn't I?"

"But I did—" Cara protested.

"No, you didn't!" Alicia exclaimed at the same time as Patty. Cara withered Patty with a look, but Alicia continued. "I heard someone say that Cara knew she'd worn it to school, and Quinn stole it. But Cara never even bothered to look for it."

"Then, Miss Antona, why didn't you tell me this?" Mrs. Hartman asked, tapping her foot against the floor.

Alicia dropped her glance. "I—I—" she began.

"Something happened I guess, sort of," she finished lamely.

"I'd say something happened," Mrs. Hartman said, her scowl deepening.

"She was only trying to help Quinn," Nicole piped up, trying to defend Alicia. "And so was Esme."

"So, Nicole, you are involved in this business, too?"

"It was all my idea," Nicole said, sounding proud of the fact. "To have Esme pretend to be Cara's friend."

Mrs. Hartman threw up her hands. "I don't want to hear the details," she said as she looked from one girl to the next. "Quinn, Nicole, Alicia, Esme, and Cara, you will stay after school for detention. I expect each of you to hand me perfectly written five-hundred-word essays first thing tomorrow morning on the importance of good behavior in school."

"Detention?" Nicole and Cara screeched.

"I can't, Mrs. Hartman," Cara protested.

"You *will*, Miss Knowles." With that, the headmistress turned on her heel and left the room.

On the way out of detention that afternoon, Quinn exclaimed to her friends, "I can't believe Cara got out of it!"

"It figures," Alicia said. "Cara Knowles in detention? Are you kidding me?"

"I know, really. How convenient that her father happened to come home from Europe today," Esme added.

"I'm really surprised," Nicole commented. "Detention's not nearly as bad as I thought it would be."

"What'd you expect, Nicole?" asked Quinn, already the detention veteran of the group. "Bars on the windows, bread and water, or what?"

"I don't know," Nicole replied, laughing. "But that essay wasn't exactly fun."

"That essay wasn't so bad. The first time Heartburn gave me detention, I had to do five hundred lines of 'I will behave with decorum and maintain the dress code at all times.' My hand almost fell off!"

"Hey, guys, I have a great idea," Esme said, changing the subject. "Let's go to Pizzarama and celebrate finally getting even with Knowles-It-All."

"Yeah, that's a good idea. I've never been there. By the way, thanks for everything, guys. I couldn't have done this by myself," Quinn said, not meeting anyone's eyes.

"That's what friends are for," Alicia replied as Esme and Nicole nodded in agreement.

"Finally," Esme exclaimed, "I can have a Pizzamania Deluxe Pie!"

*Watch for*
## PALM BEACH PREP #2
## STOLEN KISSES

**Coming Soon
from Lynx Books!**

"There's a guy on the set!" Jasmine Bartlett, an auburn-haired beauty with emerald-green eyes, exclaimed. All the models on the "Sweet Sixteen" shoot stampeded to the curtain, fighting for a glimpse.

Esme Farrell stopped buttoning her pink and white cropped top and sighed. Even if the guy was worth her attention, he'd never notice her, a sixth-grader at Palm Beach Prep and the baby of to-day's shoot.

"Stop pushing me, Beth," Kesia Murphy, a light-skinned black girl with thick, long curly hair that fell below her waist, reprimanded. Esme, who was so All-American-looking, couldn't help being a lit-tle jealous of Kesia's exotic beauty.

"Well, if you'd give me a chance to look out, I wouldn't have to push," Beth Morely retorted as she pushed her straight black bangs away from her dark blue eyes.

Esme watched the older girls as they struggled to get dressed and keep an eye on the guy outside. She had just started modeling for magazines. Kesia, Jasmine, and Beth were all much more experienced. Jasmine had even just finished doing the October cover for *Sassy,* and Kesia was scheduled to do her first adult shoot for *Mademoiselle* in December.

"C'mon, Esme. Look!" Jasmine commanded as she pulled Esme up to the curtain.

Under a pink banner with candy-striped letters that spelled "Sweet Sixteen" was a mock-up of a fifties-style soda fountain. Behind the fountain was THE GUY. He had dark curly hair and a great tan. He looked at least sixteen years old. Esme's heart stopped and then began beating so loudly she was sure he could hear it across the floor.

Susie Brickshaw, the stylist, entered the dressing room and told the girls to get a move on. By the time Esme got out there, Jasmine was already planted on a chrome-trimmed stool in front of the soda fountain. Kesia and Beth were grouped at one end of the pink formica counter.

"Okay Blondie, over there!" the photographer barked, and directed Esme to hop up on the counter and sit in front of Gregg. With a gulp, Esme obeyed.

"Hi, there, Blondie." The voice behind her was low and deep, and Esme got goose bumps on her arms.

"Until recently, Esme was 'shorty,' " Beth said, pointing at Esme. "Right, kid?" Esme had worked with Beth before, but she had never sounded so obnoxious.

"I like Blondie better," Gregg interrupted as he smiled down at Esme, "but I like Esme best of all."

"Look like you're flirting, you two," the photographer instructed them. "Make conversation. You've got the idea, Gregg. Relax, Blondie."

Esme made herself face Gregg and not for the first time wished that Palm Beach Prep was co-ed. Gregg slung his arm over her shoulder. The lights were burning, and two minutes into the shoot Esme was roasting. But Gregg's touch sent a shiver right down her spine.

"All right, Gregg," the photographer commanded, "now kiss her."

Esme's blue eyes opened very wide and she almost fell right off the counter. *My first kiss!*

## DON'T MISS ANY OF THE BOOKS IN THE VERY INCREDIBLE AND TOTALLY FUN PALM BEACH PREP SERIES

### NEW GIRL IN TOWN (Book #1)

After her first day at exclusive Palm Beach Preparatory School for Girls, it's Quinn McNair against the snobs. But tough Quinn is ready to take on the entire school all by herself, until she meets Alicia Antona, Esme Farrell, and Nicole Whitcomb.

### STOLEN KISSES (Book #2)

Modeling's no big deal for Esme Farrell, until she's on her first teenage magazine shoot and she meets Gorgeous Gregg, a sixteen-year-old male model. Her heart starts beating wildly and she almost faints when he asks her out. There's only one small problem—he thinks Esme's sixteen, too. . . .

### HEAD OF THE CLASS (Book #3)

Alicia Antona has had it with Cara Knowles-It-All and her snobby attitude. She and Cara are both running for class president and they're both determined to win. Dirty tricks are right up Cara's alley. The question is, can Alicia beat Cara at her own game?

### LONELY HEARTS (Book #4)

Nicole likes being an only child, even if her parents are divorced and her mother's not around all that much. When she finds out her mother plans to remarry and that she's going to have a stepbrother just her age, calm-and-collected Nicole blows her cool and runs away from home.

### SCREEN TEST (Book #5)

Esme's off to Hollywood for a screen test. Her new agent is sure she's going to be a star! Esme couldn't be more excited until she realizes that her agent may be more than she can handle and that life without her very best friends Alicia, Nicole, and Quinn is no fun at all.

### THE REAL SCOOP (Book #6)

Just because editor-in-chief Cara Knowles won't let Quinn write for *The Sixth Gator* isn't enough to stop Quinn. With the help of Alicia, Nicole, and Esme, she starts her own underground paper called *The Real Scoop*. And then Quinn goes a little too far and it looks like she may lose her very best friends forever. . . .